"We hear the district attorney was called to your school,"

Mrs. Dottie Dukesberry said, leaning forward in her chair.

Patience nearly dropped her glass of iced tea. "The district attorney?"

"Yes, his son is in your class. Little Darby."

"Oh." Patience hadn't realized that Gil Montgomery was the D.A.

"So what did you think of Gil?"

What had she thought of Gil Montgomery? The image of him, compact and powerful-looking, with chocolate-brown hair, tantalized Patience like a warm breath on her neck. She hid a shiver. He'd made an impression on her with his blue eyes, well-cut suit and shined wing tips. But he was the father of a student.

* * *

Books by Lyn Cote

Love Inspired

Never Alone #30
New Man in Town #66
Hope's Garden #111
Finally Home #137
Finally Found #162
The Preacher's Daughter #221
*His Saving Grace #247
*Testing His Patience #255

*Sisters of the Heart

LYN COTE

now lives in Wisconsin with her husband, her real-life hero. They raised a son and daughter together. Lyn has spent her adult life as a schoolteacher, a full-time mom and now a writer. Lyn's favorite food is watermelon. Realizing that this delicacy is only available one season out of the year, Lyn's friends keep up a constant flow of "watermelon" gifts—candles, wood carvings, pillows, cloth bags, candy and on and on. Lyn also enjoys crocheting and knitting, watching *Wheel of Fortune* and doing lunch with friends. By the way, Lyn's last name is pronounced "Coty."

Lyn enjoys hearing from readers, and they can contact her at P.O. Box 864, Woodruff, WI 54568, or by e-mail at l.cote@juno.com.

TESTING HIS PATIENCE

LYN COTE

Published by Steeple Hill Books™

STEEPLE HILL BOOKS

Steeple
Hill®

ISBN 0-373-87265-8

TESTING HIS PATIENCE

Copyright © 2004 by Lyn Cote

This edition published by arrangement with Steeple Hill Books.

® and TM are trademarks of Steeple Hill Books, used under license. Trademarks indicated with ® are registered in the United States Patent and Trademark Office, the Canadian Trade Marks Office and in other countries.

www.SteepleHill.com

Printed in U.S.A.

Forgive us our trespasses as we forgive those
who trespass against us.

—*Luke* 11:4

To my editor, Diane Dietz.
Thanks for all your cheerful help
and skillful guidance. You inspire me.

Chapter One

On a golden early-October afternoon in southern Illinois, Patience Andrews sat at her desk, her head down but her eyes roaming her first-grade classroom. She only wished she had more experience.

Last year's student teaching was a far cry from being on her own with twenty-five six- and -seven-year-olds, but it had taught her a few things. For instance, within five minutes on the first day of class, Patience had recognized that Darby Montgomery would be ''the challenge'' in her first year of teaching. Now she had to figure out how to change this, turn the boy around.

Darby's kindergarten teacher had labeled him on his student file as a ''behavior problem—needs social worker evaluation.'' Patience refused to fall into that mindset. Too often children lived up to what they were labeled. Therefore, the label should be a positive one.

That much she'd learned from Uncle Mike and Aunt Mary. "And I'll always be grateful, Lord," she murmured aloud.

With his chocolate-brown bangs and eyes to match, maybe Darby just needed extra attention.

A bouquet of bright yellow and bronze marigolds in a jelly jar, a gift from a student, graced her desk. She touched one soft petal. Then a nattering sound from the windowsill made her glance over. Outside the window, noisy squirrels were busy gathering acorns. They raced up and down the oak tree.

By contrast, inside the classroom, everyone was copying their spelling list for the week, or trying to in spite of the activity just outside their windows. The children glanced from the words on the chalkboard behind her to the paper on their desks and back again. Many had their faces twisted with intense concentration and gripped their large pencils with pressure-whitened fingertips.

One brave reddish-brown squirrel scampered onto the classroom's open windowsill and chattered louder than the rest. The children kept glancing at it and then back at their papers. Patience looked at Darby again. She was right. Darby needed extra attention.

And he needed it—right now.

Unlike his fellow first-graders, Darby, sitting three seats back on the window row, wasn't copying his spelling words. Not a surprise. He was staring at the brave and chatty squirrel. As she watched them both, he half rose from his seat. Was he going to the window?

"Class!" Patience spoke up.

Darby froze en route.

"Time for a stretch! Everybody up beside their desks!" Patience jumped from her seat and stood beside her desk. "Now, everyone stretch your hands high!"

The class grinned at her as they popped up to follow her example.

"And bend down low." Folded in two, Patience made eye contact with Darby. Did he realize she'd been watching him, anticipating him? "Now up high again."

To her eyes, he looked confused. *Good. If I can just keep one step ahead of him...*

"Very good, class." Patience let her arms drop. "You may be seated again."

The boys and girls settled back into their seats with some giggling and chatter. The bold squirrel at the window still sat on the sill of their open window, appearing intrigued by the class. This surprised Patience. Why hadn't the sudden activity scared the squirrel back into the tree?

"Spelling words, please," she reminded sternly. "We don't want to have to stay in during recess on this gorgeous day to finish them, do we?"

Murmurs of agreement preceded the resumption of intense copying. The pleasant silence of busy students blanketed the room, a sound that warmed her teacher's heart. Patience checked and saw that Darby had finally picked up his pencil. Good. Maybe now he'd get busy with his work.

In the cheery silence, from the hallway came a sudden yelp and thud. Patience jumped up and ran to the doorway. Down the hall, a silver-haired woman, the school librarian, lay upon the linoleum. She groaned.

Patience hurried forward. "Are you hurt?"

The librarian struggled to rise. Patience took her arm and helped her up.

"There must have been some water on the floor by the drinking fountain," the woman gasped. "I lost my footing—"

Sudden shrieks broke over them, echoing off the cement-brick walls. Patience spun around and raced back to her room—just in time to see Darby chasing the inquisitive squirrel around the room.

Gil Montgomery forced himself not to fidget on the straight-backed chair as he faced Mrs. Canney, the Oakdale principal. It didn't help that she had been *his* principal, too. "I don't see how a squirrel in a class-room could cause such a furor."

"That's hardly the attitude we would like you to take as Darby's father." Mrs. Canney looked at him over her half-glasses.

Right. He scrambled for an acceptable excuse. "I have a case I'm preparing." *And it's more critical than whatever's happening in a first-grade class.* "I fail to see why you insisted I come here now. It's not Darby's fault if a squirrel got in through an open window."

"The whole class agreed that Darby enticed the squirrel." Her lips drawn together like the wrong end of a prune, Mrs. Canney folded her hands on the desk and gazed at him. "Darby went to the window when Miss Andrews had left the room to help our librarian who'd fallen in the hallway. Your son got out of his seat and put a piece of candy on the sill to entice the squirrel inside."

"I don't get it. Squirrels usually run away when a human approaches them. Why didn't the squirrel just scat?" Gil let himself frown at her. *I've got too much on my mind for something petty like this.*

"You're right. This particular squirrel has grown up on the school grounds and I'm afraid children have fed it over the past few years. This makes it behave differently than your average wild squirrel."

"So it really wasn't Darby's fault."

"You're missing the point, Gilbert." Mrs. Canney shook her head at him, the loose skin under her neck swaying. "Darby or some other student could easily have been bitten. And I don't think you'd like him or any child to have to go through the series of rabies shots if that had happened and we hadn't been able to find the squirrel.''

Gil realized he was gritting his teeth and relaxed his jaw. ''But he didn't get bitten. No one did.''

''Darby is too young to be doing this type of stunt,'' Mrs. Canney snapped. ''This is a fourth-grader prank, not a first-grader prank.''

This stumped Gil. Was that a compliment or an insult?

''Now, I want you to take Darby home and talk to him about wild animals and why contact with them should be avoided.'' Mrs. Canney pressed the button on her intercom. ''Please send Darby in.''

Darby, his head down, opened the door and edged inside the room. A tall willowy blonde entered behind his son. Gil noticed that she had rested her hand on his son's shoulder. Was she restraining Darby or comforting him? Gil rose. He couldn't stop himself from running his gaze over the woman. Very attractive. Very young. Very unsettling.

''Gil, this is Miss Andrews, Darby's teacher,'' Mrs. Canney introduced them.

Miss Andrews offered him her hand.

He took it—so light and delicate—in his. The unusual sensation made him break contact. He tried to read the teacher's expression. He failed.

Mrs. Canney shot Darby a stern look and then extended it to include Gil. ''Darby, I'm letting your father take you home now. But starting tomorrow, you will spend recess sitting in my office and you will have to stay after school and clean chalkboards for Miss Andrews for the rest of the week.''

''No recess,'' Darby muttered, jamming his hands into his pockets.

Gil squeezed his son's shoulder. ''No back talk. Apologize to Mrs. Canney for making trouble.''

''I'm sorry.'' Darby stared at the gray carpet.

''I'm sure—'' Miss Andrews looked to Gil. ''—Darby didn't realize that a squirrel might be a danger to the other students.''

''Now he does.'' Mrs. Canney picked up a paper from her desk, dismissing them. ''Thank you for coming in, Gilbert.''

Gil mumbled something, preoccupied with his own thoughts. Miss Andrews's voice had caught Gil by surprise. What could make a voice that rich and low?

He let Miss Andrews and his son precede him out the door. The three of them walked down the shadowy, empty hallway. The teacher held herself very straight, and was tall enough to be just inches beneath his own height. He tried to keep his eyes forward, but they kept tracking right to her profile.

An awkward situation. Gil tried to think of something to say to make her speak again, to hear her voice again. But he could come up with nothing. He didn't want to talk about Darby's indiscretion until he'd had time to speak to his son in private. And every other thought in his mind referenced the Putnam case.

They reached the main school entrance. He started to say goodbye but stopped.

Miss Andrews had lowered herself to sit on her heels, her nose only inches from his son's. "Darby, I know you didn't mean to do something that might hurt you or someone else. But you've got to start thinking things out first, okay?"

"Are you mad at me?" Darby asked in a little voice.

"No, I'm not mad. I'm sad."

"Why?" Darby looked up for the first time.

"Because you ended up frightening that little squirrel when you chased him—"

"I was just trying to catch him so he could get back outside. I didn't think he'd come in for the candy..."

"You must think before you do things. The squirrel didn't deserve what happened, to be terrified, did he?" Miss Andrews touched Darby's cheek with the back of her hand.

Gil felt the phantom of this touch on his own cheek. What would it feel like to have Miss Andrews speaking to him nose to nose? *Stupid question.* And it caused his face to warm. He remained in the shadows, a step apart, made mute by this stranger's compassion to his son.

"Does terrified mean I scared him?" Darby's voice quivered and he moved an inch closer to Miss Andrews.

"Yes. The poor little squirrel didn't deserve to have

people screaming at him and chasing him. Just think how little he is and how big we all looked to him. It was like putting him in a scary movie with huge monsters, only it was real.''

"I didn't mean to scare him." Darby's voice vibrated with true regret.

Gil realized he'd been holding his breath and exhaled.

"I know you didn't. But next time, think first." She ruffled Darby's hair and then rose in one swift fluid movement that again caught Gil off guard. She offered Gil her hand again. "Goodbye."

He closed his own over her slight hand, still unable to think of a thing to say. "Thanks" didn't seem adequate.

She turned and he watched her walk back up the dim, cavernous hall. The feminine swing of her body captured his attention. He couldn't break away until the shadows obscured her from his view.

His son tugged on his hand. "Come on, Dad."

"Right." He let Darby lead him out into the molten sunshine of late afternoon, forcing himself to keep his face forward. And hiding his eyes behind his light-sensitive glasses.

Patience paused at the corner and sighed. The afternoon gossip group lounged on Mrs. Honeycutt's front porch where Patience rented the upper flat. No way out. She'd stop and chat a few moments, avoiding any gossip and then head upstairs. On such a warm day, she had only one compelling thing on her mind: taking off her hose and slipping into shorts would be heaven.

She'd been lucky to find such a nice apartment in the small community. From this street of vintage Victorian houses, she walked the few blocks to Oakdale School every day. Overhead, the hundred-year-old maples flamed, side-by-side with bronzed oak leaves. But away from the shade of the tall trees, sun still dazzled the eyes and the summer heat lingered.

Patience breathed in deeply and felt the tension of the day begin to disappear from her. She opened the picket gate and started up the walk to the gathering on the porch.

"Patience!" her landlady, Bunny Honeycutt, called out. "You're late! Long day?"

Patience smiled. She couldn't be cross with Bunny, a woman reminiscent of Aunt Bea in Mayberry, with the same silver hair and bun, but who preferred blue jeans and a strict diet to keep herself thin. An Aunt Bea updated for the twenty-first century.

Bunny handed Patience her clutch of mail.

"Tea?" Greta Overwood, a tall woman who wore her steel-gray hair cut in a Dutch boy and who favored wearing her late husband's clothing, held up an empty pint-glass jar.

"Yes, a glass of iced tea would hit the spot." Patience sank into a weathered wicker chair with a frayed cushion. The wicker creaked, a pleasant sound. She let the mail drop into her lap. A little dog yipped next door.

"We hear the district attorney was called to your school." Mrs. Dottie Dukesberry, a well-cushioned woman who always wore bright colors, leaned forward in her chair.

Patience nearly dropped the glass of tea Greta had just handed her. She stared at Dottie, who today sported bright pink slacks and a pink blouse. "The district attorney?"

"Yes, his son is in your class." Bunny handed Patience a paper napkin. "Little Darby."

"Oh." Patience thought of what to say next while she sipped the icy tea. She hadn't realized that Gil was the D.A. The local rumor mill must be active if his visit was already *on the street*. "Yes, he was."

"What happened?" Dottie asked in a distinctive sweet, breathy voice, edging farther forward on her seat.

Greta shook her head and grumbled something under her breath.

"Now, Dottie," Bunny said in a placating tone, "the boy is only in first grade. What could he have done that would be so awful?"

"You're just sweet on his grandfather, the Captain," Dottie said with a sly look at Bunny.

"It wasn't serious." Ignoring the innuendo, Patience let herself relax into the comfortable chair.

Bunny's large gold tabby cat, Jonesy, hopped up onto her lap. "A squirrel came in the window and Darby tried to catch him. Mrs. Canney was just concerned that Darby didn't realize that the squirrel might have bitten him."

She stroked Jonesy's velvet ears. "Then he might have had to go through those awful rabies shots."

"What did you think of Gil Montgomery?" Dottie asked, the afternoon sun glinting on her wire-rim glasses.

What had she thought of Gil Montgomery? The image of him, compact and powerful-looking with the same chocolate-brown hair as Darby, tickled Patience like a warm breath on her nape. She hid a shiver. "We didn't really have a chance to talk—"

"What did you *think* of him?" Dottie demanded with a snap in her Southern belle voice. "I wasn't talking about *talking*."

Greta snorted and shook her head, her severe Dutch bangs swishing over her grooved forehead.

Patience sipped her sweet tea and stroked Jonesy. She'd heard about small-town gossip and here she sat in the midst of it. Gil Montgomery had made an impression on her with his blue eyes, well-cut suit and shined wingtips. But he was the father of a student. Dottie's avid tone warned Patience to be cagey. "He seemed very nice."

"Nice!" Dottie exclaimed. "If I were thirty years younger—"

"Gil Montgomery would be dodging you." Bunny chortled with an impish light in her eyes. "Just like the Captain does."

Dottie ignored Bunny. "I know you're from Chicago, but you would have to go some distance to find a man as eligible as Gil Montgomery."

"But he's divorced and has that little boy," Greta added in her raspy voice. "For a first marriage, a girl's better off not getting a man with entanglements *and* a history."

"It's not his fault he's divorced," Bunny said. "We all know his wife divorced him against his will and for no good reason."

"They never should have got married in the first place," Greta huffed. "Different as night and day."

Patience sipped her iced tea, trying not to let any of this talk sink in. Gossip would be unreliable at best. She'd like to ask someone about Darby, but not at the price of making Dottie think she had an interest in his handsome father. Still lounging in her lap, Jonesy began purring like a small engine.

"I bet Gil wasn't happy having to cut his day short." Greta crossed her legs, her late husband's jeans bagging at her knees. "That Putnam trial is coming up fast."

"Mmm. Now *that* was a bad business." Bunny pushed the plate of chocolate chip cookies toward Patience. "I was up at the Rose Care Center this morning to visit Bertha. She still can't walk or speak a word.''

''It just breaks my heart to see her that way.'' Dottie patted her sixties' bubble hairstyle. ''And to think it might have been her son that did it to her.''

Glad that the Gil inquiry had been shelved, Patience put down her tea on the glass-topped wicker table and drew her mail from under Jonesy's white-furred tummy. The cat blinked up at her. Patience sorted through the letters, mostly credit card applications and car insurance offers. *I don't want to be in debt and I don't own a car.*

''I don't believe Bertha Perkins was attacked by family,'' Bunny snapped. ''Dan had his problems but I don't think he would ever hurt anyone.''

At the bottom of her pile of mail, an official-looking envelope caught Patience's eye. She ran her finger under the flap of the thick, expensive paper and opened it.

''He tried to hurt himself.'' Greta picked up the fly swatter resting on her lap and followed the progress of a large housefly circling over the cookies.

''That's over thirty years ago.'' Bunny's voice starched up. ''We didn't know as much then as we do now about people with mental illness. Oprah just had a show about that.''

''*Oh.*'' The official letter forced the muted exclamation from Patience. She wanted to add ''No,'' but swallowed it. She looked up and all three women stared at her.

"I don't think you better say any more about that case," Patience said, an odd constriction making her work to force out the words.

"Why, dear?" Dottie asked, her nose drawing even closer to Patience.

"Because I've just been called for jury duty."

Chapter Two

Hearing her name called, loud and brusque, by the bailiff at the door of the courtroom, Patience rose from a bench in the crowded hallway. Other prospective jurors grouped around gave her assessing looks. She averted her eyes.

Over the weekend, she'd read up on jury selection, or in jurisprudence jargon, *voir dire*. And what she'd read hadn't boosted her lagging enthusiasm about being chosen to serve on a jury. But would she have a choice?

With her spine straight, she walked inside the nearly empty courtroom, her heart doing a violent jig. Only subdued murmurs from the lawyers and the furious buzzing of a fly trying to get out a closed window broke the silence.

I don't want to be in court again—for any reason.

Though the nervous habit of biting her nails was trying to ensnare her, she forced herself to keep her
hands at her sides. Images from her past reared up—
a courtroom in Chicago, lawyers arguing over her as
though she weren't even there listening to every word.
An echo of the helpless fury she'd felt then flashed
through her like a string of firecrackers.

From the corner of her eye, she glimpsed Gil Montgomery alone at one of the two counsel tables. His
confident stance and air of assurance contrasted
sharply with her own jelly-kneed hesitancy. Then he
looked up, meeting her eyes and something like an
electric charge zipped through her.

Across the aisle from him, a stranger talked to a
thin man with a salt-and-pepper mustache and dressed
in an orange uniform. *That must be the defendant and
his lawyer. I didn't know I'd have to face Dan Putnam
today.*

She followed the bailiff's instructions and proceeded to take her place behind the rail at the witness
stand. A once-over glance told her that the courtroom
looked like most courtrooms—walls of polished oak
paneling mirrored in a hardwood floor, high nineteenth-century plastered ceilings and the U.S. and Illinois flags flanking the front where she stood.

"Raise your left hand," the bailiff said in a bored
monotone. "Do you have any objection to swearing
on the Bible?"

"No." *I have an objection to being here.*

"Then place your right hand on the Bible and repeat after me—'I swear to tell the whole truth and nothing but the truth, so help me God.'"

Patience found it hard to take breath. But she repeated the words that echoed in the vast, intimidating room. *Please, God, get me out of this. It's too hard. It brings back too many memories. Please.* She let herself down onto the seat, hearing the chair under her creak, a loud sound in the silent room. Then she didn't know where to look. Her eyes wanted to linger on Gil Montgomery, the one familiar face in the room.

But she wouldn't focus on him. Not after their less-than-pleasant meeting at school last week. Not in this situation which she knew demanded impartiality. And not when she kept noticing the endearing cleft in his chin that belied his serious expression and gave him a touch of vulnerability. *Don't go there. He's off-limits.*

"Miss Andrews, you are a teacher at Oakdale School?" Gil asked her in an official-sounding voice.

She cleared her dry throat. "Yes."

"Do you know of any reason that you are not fit to be a member of the jury in this case?" Gil looked at her as if she were a stranger.

Why? Had she made no impression on him at all? "I'm not clear on what that means exactly," Patience hedged.

"Primarily, it means—" Gil's voice was sharp

"—have you already formed an opinion about the accused's guilt or innocence?"

Patience waited a moment before responding, letting him know she wouldn't be rushed or bullied. She faced him squarely then, resisting the urge to look into his blue eyes behind his black, wire-rim glasses. "No. I'm new around here. I don't know Mrs. Perkins or her son." *I know your son. Does that make a difference?*

"But you do know that Dan Putnam is the victim's son?" the defendant's lawyer, Sprague, spoke for the first time. He was much older than Gil, with white hair and a noticeable paunch.

"Yes—" Patience fanned her fingers over her lap, pressing her fingertips down to keep her nails away from her mouth "—I have read the local paper and have heard some talk."

"But you haven't formed an opinion about this case?" Gil took a step around the desk as though ready to advance toward her.

"No, I haven't." Looking away from Gil, Patience glanced up at the judge, an attractive man in his middle years. "But I don't feel I'm qualified to judge another person's guilt or innocence." She refused to glance at Gil and see the response to this in his expression.

The judge frowned down on her. "As a citizen, you are only asked to listen to the evidence and make a reasonable decision based on that evidence. We don't expect prescience.''

Patience gathered her spunk. *I have to let the judge know.* "Should I mention that I'm the teacher of the district attorney's son?''

The judge glanced toward Gil and then back to her. "I don't think that is enough of a connection to show partiality. What does counsel for the defense think?''

Behind the cover of the railing, Patience crossed fingers on both hands. *Please, Lord, let him say he doesn't want me. I don't think it's good for me to be around Gil when I'm Darby's teacher. And when I'm having so much trouble ignoring him as a man.*

"I don't think that's much of a connection,'' Sprague agreed, rocking back on his heels.

"Do you think,'' Gil went on as if she and Sprague hadn't spoken, "there is anything in your background which would preclude your serving as an impartial juror in this case?''

"Like what?'' Patience tried to think. Should she tell him about Chicago? *No.*

"Have you or someone close to you been charged with a similar crime?'' Gil stared at her with pursed lips.

"No.'' *No, I wasn't guilty of assault and robbery.*

"I have no objections to accepting Miss Andrews,'' Sprague commented, looking at his notes, not at her.

Gil stared into her eyes, a long searching look.

It made her twice as aware of him as she had been.

The hair on her arms prickled as though he were drawing near. "I believe I'd be more useful back in my classroom," she ventured. *Darby needs me. I don't think he'll get along with my substitute. He needs consistency and I don't want him to get a reputation as class clown or—*

"I have no objection to accepting Miss Andrews." Gil looked away.

She felt dismissed and more puzzled. *Which is most unsettling to me, this awkward situation or Gil Montgomery?*

"Bailiff, show Miss Andrews to the room where the jurors are waiting." The judge waved his hand.

Lost in confusion over this outcome, Patience rose as though unseen hands had lifted the strings that controlled her and she followed the bailiff through a doorway on one side of the courtroom.

I've had enough of courtrooms to last me a lifetime. Now I'm going to be forced to come into this courtroom again—for days, maybe weeks. A hollow feeling made her feel a bit nauseated. *How did that happen so fast? Why didn't either of them eliminate me? I don't want to be on a jury. I don't want to face Gil Montgomery every day.*

At ten o'clock the next morning, Gil kept his focus forward on the judge, who was formally impaneling the jury that had been chosen for the Putnam case. This swearing in of the jury was routine; however,

Gil's keen awareness of Miss Patience Andrews was not routine.

Tall, blond and impossible to ignore, she stood on the far right in the first row of the jury box. Her presence added a whole new dimension to the usual tumultuous emotions that bubbled up inside him at the start of each new trial.

I should have recused her. I do have a connection, though tenuous, to her. And what did she mean, "I believe I'd be more useful back in my classroom?" Did she mean Darby needed her?

Thinking of Darby and school made his resentment at his ex-wife and her mishandling of their son rear up. It was an itch he couldn't scratch—not yet. The frustration that had hovered just beneath his consciousness all last night now flooded through him again, hot and straining to be released. *Doesn't she care at all about our son's future?*

The jury en masse finished repeating their oath and sat down with much scraping of chairs and a brief rumble of polite comments.

It's too late now. I'm stuck with Miss Patience Andrews on the jury.

Gil stepped around his table and addressed the court with his prepared opening. "This trial will decide whether Daniel Putnam did or did not assault and attack his mother on August 22 of this year in Cole County. The state believes that Daniel Putnam is guilty of striking his mother with blunt force, which made her lose consciousness and later to suffer a stroke. The state believes that Daniel Putnam did this with the intent to steal money and valuable antiques from his mother's home.''

He felt Patience focusing on him. Was it him as a man or was she concentrating on him as district attorney? And why did he care?

He proceeded to set up the case against Putnam. Then, after listening to Sprague's opening comments, Gil called his first witness, the arresting officer.

A tall lanky man in his forties, Sheriff Longworthy took the oath and began to answer questions.

''Why did you go to the home of Mrs. Bertha Perkins located at 202 Walnut Street on the night of August 22 of this year?'' Gil asked the routine question. But somehow his usual in-court confidence felt compromised. Out of the corner of his eye, he noted that Patience Andrews also appeared strained, uncomfortable.

I should have sent her back to her classroom. She's distracting me. Why did I insist she be here as part of the jury? Maybe he just liked looking at her too much.

''I got a call from one of her roomers.'' The sheriff looked down at his notebook. ''One Wade Bevin, forty-two, who has rented a room at Mrs. Perkins's almost three years. He called me when he arrived home and found Mrs. Perkins on her kitchen floor unconscious. I immediately called the paramedics and we both arrived at the residence about the same time.'' Another glance at his notebook. ''I arrived at 12:23 a.m. right before the EMTs arrived.''

Gil went on prompting the sheriff to give the bare facts of the crime scene.

Out of the blue, his thoughts took him back to last night when he'd overheard Darby laughing with a friend about the squirrel incident—''My mommy says that she wished she was there to see me chasing that squirrel!''

Gil's temper ignited all over again. Hot words had been running through his mind all night and morning. The blistering words had cycled again and again, refusing to be tabled, words about what he thought of his ex-wife's behavior, her careless attitudes.

When Darby had left Friday evening, he had been repentant about the squirrel and wanting to do better at school in the coming week. Why had Coreena changed the misdemeanor into a funny escapade? Didn't she know that would only make Darby more likely to get into trouble? *All the good I try to do with Darby goes up in smoke every other weekend when he's with his mother.*

The sheriff's testimony drew to a close and he stepped down. Gil gritted his teeth. He'd lay down the law once and for all. But with Coreena that was easier said than done.

A bailiff came from the back of the courtroom and passed Gil a slip of paper. He read it:

Gilbert, I thought you should know that Darby's mother came in this morning and took him out of school for the day.

Sincerely,
Mrs. Canney.

Anger scalded Gil's stomach. *She knew she could get away with this because I'd be tied up in court. That's it. The final straw.*

Later Tuesday afternoon after court had adjourned, Gil got out of his sedan, slammed the door and marched toward the trailer where his ex-wife lived. She wouldn't get away with this. Not again.

The trailer was new, a double-wide with a satellite dish on top. That was another thing he wanted stopped—Darby watching cable channels he shouldn't be watching. His child wouldn't suffer because of his careless mother.

Gil hammered on the door. "Coreena! It's Gil."

Darby opened the door. "Hi, Dad!"

Gil frowned down at his son. "Is your mother here?"

"'Course, I'm here. You don't think I'd leave the kid all alone, do you?" Coreena came into view wearing white short-shorts and a purple halter top.

"Darby, will you please go outside and sit in

the car?'' Gil asked as he pulled his son through the open door.

"You better go, hon," Coreena said in a lazy voice. "Your dad wants to tell me off and doesn't want you to have to listen to it."

"But, Mommy—"

Burning at Coreena's flippant put-down, Gil turned Darby to face the car. "Wait outside. Then your mom will come out and say goodbye."

Gil stepped inside and let the door close behind him. "What do you mean taking Darby out of school without my permission?"

Coreena gave him a long-suffering sigh. "I got the day off unexpectedly and decided to go shopping in Marion. Just wanted some company. Darby and I had a great time. McDonald's for lunch and hot pretzels and mustard at the mall."

"Per our custody agreement, you don't have the authority to take Darby out of school on a whim. If you do this again, I'll designate that only I have the right to take Darby out of school." Gil controlled himself, struggling to sound calm.

"Oh, Gil, what's the big deal? I haven't done it before and I probably won't do it again any time soon. It was just such a beautiful fall day and I wanted to spend it with Darby."

Her petite figure and tousled brown hair with blond highlights and big brown eyes still added up to an attractive woman but not to him. Not anymore. The I-was-just-being-a-fun-mom argument wasn't without its charm, either. Under normal conditions, her behavior wouldn't have been outrageous. But knowing her attitude toward school and the way her comments might egg Darby on...

"Coreena," Gil said in his sternest tone, "Darby is having problems getting settled down in first grade. He should have been there today, serving detention in the principal's office for—"

"Yeah, I know. The squirrel stunt." She shrugged. "What's the big deal over letting a squirrel in school? What is this, 'Mary Had a Little Lamb' or something?"

The nursery rhyme reference took him a moment to connect with the topic at hand. He grimaced at being sidetracked. "If the squirrel had bitten someone, especially our son, your attitude would be really different."

"But it didn't, so it's a big deal over nothing." Coreena perched on the arm of her couch, swinging one shapely tanned leg back and forth. "That old Mrs. Canney is past it if you ask me—"

"No one asked you," Gil snapped. "It is irresponsible for you to encourage Darby to disobey his teacher and principal. Do you want him to get labeled as a troublemaker? Do you think you'll be doing him a favor?"

"Who starched your boxers? Just because I have a sense of humor and Old Lady Canney doesn't—"

Gil's temper flashed white-hot again. "You pull

something like this again and I'm going to sue to end your visitation rights.''

Coreena stood up, folding her arms in front of her. ''I was good enough for you once, you know. That kid is *ours,* not just yours. I let you have full custody of him, as long as you stayed around here. I don't care if you are the D.A., you're not taking away my time with my son. Period.''

''Is he going to stay much longer? I want to go get somethin' to eat.'' A tall, very muscular man walked out from the bedroom. He wore his dishwater-blond hair in a ponytail and the arms of his shirt had been ripped out. All the better to display his Harley tattoo on his upper right arm and skull and serpent on his left.

Gil stared at him.

''Oh, Gil, this is the new man in my life, Blaine Cody.''

Gil automatically put out his hand.

Blaine gripped it tight, tight enough to cause Gil discomfort. ''Hear you're the local D.A.'' The man taunted Gil with a mocking grin. ''D.A.'s and me don't usually get along much.''

The second day of the trial, Patience sat up straighter in her chair in the jury box as the district attorney called another witness to the stand. The man gave his name as Wade Bevin, who lived at the same address as Mrs. Perkins.

"You have rented a room from Mrs. Perkins for over two years," Gil Montgomery asked.

"Yes, sir, almost three years." The man shifted in his seat. Patience didn't blame him. The witness chair was a hot seat even for innocent witnesses.

"You are the person who discovered that Mrs. Perkins had been attacked?" Gil looked at a legal pad on the table before him.

Patience's sympathy stirred. How awful for this man to have seen his landlady like that.

"Yeah," Wade replied, glancing up at the judge, "I came home from a job—I do handyman work for several widows here in town—and I found Mrs. Perkins on the kitchen floor. A real shock."

"Did you see anyone fleeing the residence?" Darby's dad asked.

"No, whoever done it had left. Mrs. Perkins looked bad so I called 911 right off. At first, I thought she'd just fallen and hit her head, but then I seen that stuff in the livin' room had been torn up."

Patience wondered how Darby was faring at school today. She wished for the thousandth time she was in her classroom and not this jury box.

The rest of Bevin's testimony was a repeat of what the sheriff had found when he arrived. Then Sprague asked a few minor questions and the witness stepped down.

The D.A. called his next witness for the prosecution. Patience sized up Vincent Caruthers as he took the oath and then sat down. The man was portly and middle-aged, with a pencil-thin mustache, dressed in an obviously well-cut suit.

"Mr. Caruthers," Gil said, "please state your occupation for the court."

"I am an antique dealer. I own the Shop on the Square here in Rushton."

"Do you do appraisals?"

"Yes." The man fussed with his tie.

"Did you ever do one for Mrs. Bertha Perkins?"

"Yes." Caruthers looked unhappy. "Her son called me and arranged for me to visit Mrs. Perkins at her home."

"And what did you find?"

"I found that she had several very expensive items."

"Was Mrs. Perkins interested in selling her possessions?" Gil stepped away from the prosecution table and walked toward the witness.

"No. Her son tried to persuade her, but she wouldn't agree."

Patience noted that the juror beside her was nodding as though agreeing with the antique dealer. But Patience couldn't see anything negative about the man's testimony.

"That's all the questions I have." Gil turned and walked back to his associate.

Sprague declined to ask any questions for the defense.

Patience stifled a yawn behind her hand. For all the excitement Bunny's friends had shown over the trial, Patience couldn't come up with any real interest in this unhappy crime. No one looked really like a suspect to her.

Two days later, Sprague began his defense of Dan Putnam. So far, the evidence—which had been purely circumstantial as far as Patience was concerned—had been straightforward.

Now Sprague the white-haired attorney, called his first witness, Hank Drulow, to the stand.

Patience wondered who this witness would be.

"Mr. Drulow," Sprague started, "you rent a room at Mrs. Perkins's house?"

"Yes, been there about six months." The man didn't meet Sprague's eyes.

"Was Mrs. Perkins aware that you have a criminal record?"

The witness looked chagrined and didn't respond.

"Answer the question, Mr. Drulow," the judge instructed.

"That was a long time ago and I didn't think she needed to know." Drulow sounded angry. "I wasn't intending on stealing anything if that's what you're getting at."

"But you have served time for burglary?"

"Yes, but that was over twenty years ago. I've been clean since."

Patience felt sorry for Drulow. Some stains never faded. She knew that firsthand.

Sprague's second witness was another man, a neighbor of Mrs. Perkins, Cal Fiskus, a bachelor in his thirties.

"Yes," Cal replied, "my hobby is collectibles and antiques."

"You have several times made Mrs. Perkins offers on many of her possessions?"

"Yes, I have. That's not against the law, is it?" Fiskus snapped.

"No need to be hostile. Did Mrs. Perkins ever agree to sell you any items?"

"Yes, a year ago—" the witness glanced at the jury "—she agreed to sell me her grandfather's desk."

Patience thought Sprague was doing a good job of throwing suspicion onto others.

"How much did you pay her?" Sprague asked.

"No money ever changed hands." Fiskus relaxed against the back of the chair. Was he trying to show that he wasn't intimidated? "She backed out of the deal."

"So you went away disappointed?"

"Yeah, but not disappointed enough to steal the desk. And it wasn't stolen, was it?"

Sprague concluded his interrogation of the witness and Patience thought he was doing an excellent job. Just because Dan had fought with his mother didn't really tip the scale toward him, did it?

* * *

A week after the jury had been selected, Patience sat in court, feeling sick with foreboding. Today the courtroom windows had been opened wide because of the sultry October heat. Ceiling fans swished the heavy air. Perspiration dotted Patience's upper lip and she blotted it with a tissue.

Gil had just started his summation of the case against Dan Putnam.

"Now, it has been testified to that Dan Putnam was having financial problems." Gil surveyed the jury.

Patience tried not to behave as if she noticed his marked tendency to look at her and then glance away as if he were committing a crime by noticing her. Cardboard paddle-type fans had been supplied them and she waved one at her face.

"In fact," Gil continued, "he has admitted that he is facing bankruptcy. He wanted his mother to loan him money or sell family heirlooms to help him get out of the financial bind he found himself in. A powerful motive."

Patience saw the woman juror beside her nodding and she clenched her hand around the wooden handle of the fan.

"In fact, on the evening of the attack, the disagreement between Dan and his mother got to the point where neighbors overheard them on Mrs. Perkins's back porch arguing loudly about money." Gil paused, a dour expression lengthening his face.

So what? Families fight all the time. This thought caught Patience up short. A throwback from the past. A past she wanted to forget, to live down.

In contrast to the home she'd been raised in, there hadn't been quarreling at Uncle Mike's house. Just laughter and hugs. For some reason, Patience felt the tug of tears in the back of her throat. *It must be having to sit in a courtroom again day after day. I hate this.*

"Dan Putnam was seen stomping out of the house and speeding away, obviously very angry." Gil walked closer to the jury as if confiding in them.

Anger doesn't mean anything. Being mad isn't a crime. She heard her own voice in the past screaming obscenities, cursing, and slamming the door as she ran from her mom's house.

"There was no evidence of forced entry." Gil stood before the jury, a hand on the rail in front of Patience. "That means that either Mrs. Perkins let her attacker in or her attacker had a key of his own. Again, I suggest, this points to her son."

Patience glanced down at Gil's capable-looking hand against the mellow oak. She drew in a sharp breath. *Very weak argument, Mr. District Attorney. Mrs. Perkins has two men rooming in her house. They had keys, too. Besides, who locks their doors in Rushton before bedtime?*

"We don't have the kind of community that suffers this type of crime," Gil said. "The evidence tells us this wasn't a crime perpetrated by a stranger. And from testimony accepted into evidence, Dan Putnam has been institutionalized twice in his life for bipolar disorder or manic-depression. At the very least, Dan Putnam's mental state has been proven unsettled.''

Gil paused, gazing with assurance at her and her fellow jurors—as if, no one could possibly disagree with him.

Don't count on that. Patience fanned her face more, idly reading the advertisement on it for the local funeral home.

''The state believes that we have proved that Dan Putnam, unstable mentally and under great stress because of financial problems, broke under the pressure and *struck* out at his mother. Fortunately, Mrs. Perkins survived the attack. So I ask you to bring in a verdict of guilty on the charges of assault, battery and robbery for Daniel Putnam. Thank you.''

Patience's stomach churned with her reaction to Gil's words. How could Gil think he'd proved his case? Flushing with irritation, she fanned harder.

Sprague stood up and faced the judge. ''My summation will be shorter than the district attorney's. The police have not found one witness or one scintilla of hard evidence that Dan Putnam did anything that evening except have a loud argument with his mother. Yes, he has a history of mental illness, but he is on his medication and has never been deemed a danger to others. Yes, he has had some money problems. That also isn't a crime. Yes, he argued with his mother. Who hasn't?''

Sprague stepped into the aisle and faced the jury. ''The state's case is just one string of innuendo and the barest circumstantial evidence. Dan Putnam wasn't the only one who wanted his mother to sell her valuables or who had access to her and her valuables. The sheriff was confronted with a case where there wasn't any hard evidence to convict anyone.

''But because of public outcry, he had to come up with someone to prosecute. So he picked Mrs. Perkins's son because everyone knows he tried to commit suicide thirty years ago, argued with his mother and left town. This trial has been a farce from the moment it began and I hope you will go to the jury room and let Dan Putnam, an innocent victim of small-town prejudice, go free. As he should. Thank you.''

Patience felt her burden lighten. *I couldn't have said it better myself.*

The judge gave a few very sobering final instructions and dismissed the jury to the room for deliberation. Patience filed into the same room where she had waited a week ago while the rest of the jury had been chosen. She took a seat at a long polished maple table in the center of the room.

The jury foreman looked down the length of the table and smiled. ''This shouldn't take long. Do you want to bother writing down our votes or just take a vote by a raise of hands?''

"I think we should write the votes down the first time," a gray-haired man said. "That's more official."

No one made any comment to this. Just a flurry of glances and then everyone looked to the foreman.

"Sure. Why not?" the foreman agreed affably. He passed out sheets he'd ripped one by one from a yellow legal pad along with cheap pens from a cup at the head of the table.

Patience wrote her vote down, folded the sheet and passed it forward.

The foreman received the papers and read them out one by one: "Guilty, Guilty, Guilty, Guilty, Guilty, Guilty, Guilty, Guilty, Guilty, Not Guilty, Guilty, Guilty."

Surprise and shock buzzed up and down the table.

The foreman frowned at them. "What's the deal? I thought we could wind this up in an hour."

Patience felt herself break out in a cold sweat. *This can't be happening. I can't believe they all voted guilty. What are they thinking?*

Chapter Three

Burnished copper sunshine poured through the window in the deliberation room. With agitated flicks of his wrist, the foreman sorted yet another round of ragged yellow ballots into two piles, one with many and the other with one lone vote. Fixing them all with a belligerent glare, he leaned over and braced both his hands on the table. "There is still one person, one holdout who won't go along with the majority."

His frustration, anger really, glistened on his perspiration-slick face. "What's the matter with one of you? We can't get this over with until we come to an agreement. We've gone over all the evidence twice and voted seven times and it never changes. Eleven guiltys and one not guilty!"

"Maybe we should tell the bailiff that we're at an impasse." The silver-haired man who'd earlier suggested the written ballots waved his hand as though doing a conjuring trick.

Patience clenched one hand inside the other in her lap. So far the fact that she was the odd woman out hadn't become apparent to her fellow jurors.

All day, however, the pressure had mounted and mounted in the room. After the first ballot, the jury members had started glancing at each other with one question plain on their faces: "Who's voting against the majority?" But now it had progressed to: "Who's being an irritating thorn in our side?"

Patience looked down at her hands again. "Why does it have to be so hot?" she murmured and pressed a tissue to her moist temples.

"It's you, isn't it?" the plump woman next to Patience accused in a razor-sharp tone. "You're the reason we've been sitting here hour after sweltering hour."

Patience stiffened. What she'd dreaded had come at last. What should she say? Could she speak anything but what she really thought?

Across from Patience, a middle-aged woman who obviously used boxed tint on her too-black hair squinted at her. The woman had been sending suspicious glances at Patience for the past few hours. "That's right." Her tone full of innuendo, she said, "Everyone else looks angry. You look…frozen." She pointed a finger at Patience. "You're the holdout. Don't try to deny it."

"Deny it?" Patience bristled at the thought that she would speak less than the truth. "Why should I?" Her own frustration spilled out. "What's wrong with you people? We've gone over the evidence, but with what result? None of you get it."

"What don't we get?" the foreman said through gritted teeth, deepening his pained voice. He stared down the length of the table, his face twisted in resentment.

"It's all circumstantial." Patience rose from her chair. "The D.A. doesn't have one piece of real proof against Dan Putnam—not a fingerprint, not a witness—"

"The neighbors heard them arguing," the silver-haired gentleman cut her off.

"So what?" Patience reveled in finally being able to voice her opinion. Fervor flowed out within her words. "Haven't any of you had a loud argument with a family member? I would think that if Dan Putnam were going to hurt his mother, he would have avoided calling attention to himself."

"Dan's had mental problems!" the middle-aged woman blustered. "He doesn't think like a normal person."

"You don't know what you're talking about." Patience's reply snapped like razor-sharp teeth in the tense room. "Just because a person has a history of mental illness doesn't mean they can't reason. And if you are going to use his mental problems against him, then you *can't* hold him responsible for his actions *if* his illness has so completely debilitated him."

Taut silence bound the table, froze all movement, all reaction, except for Patience's. She stood even straighter and challenged them one by one with a fierce look.

The other jurors avoided her eyes. A minute, two minutes, three minutes passed with the ticking of the antique wall clock with its swinging pendulum.

"That's it, then?" The foreman's rough voice sounded as though he were dragging it up from a dark cave. "You won't change your mind?"

Every eye was upon her. She took a deep breath. "When the D.A. gives me one shred of real evidence—" Patience glared at the man, at them all "—and not small-town prejudice, I'll change my vote. Until then, *never.*"

At her words, the rigid silence became charged with palpable antagonism. She'd just called them small-town and prejudiced. *I don't care, Lord. It's the truth.*

On Saturday afternoon, three days after the Putnam trial had ended in a mistrial, Gil stood in his backyard on another warm October day. He pitched a softball to Darby. The fastball whipped past Darby and the boy ran to pick it up.

"Sorry," Gil apologized.

"That's okay." Darby threw the ball back.

Gil caught it as it smacked his catcher's mitt. He

flexed his shoulder muscles, trying to loosen the tension that refused to leave him. He'd hoped a day off with Darby would give him release from the stress of the past week. But neither Darby's eager face nor the beauty of the perfect fall day pushed away the feeling he had. His defeat pained him like a bruise he kept bumping.

What was the use? He'd been too busy for weeks preparing the Putnam case to spend time like this with Darby. *Now I'll have to do it all over again.*

Still smoldering, Gil took aim and pitched again, but this time a low easy ball.

Darby ran forward and grabbed the ball just before it hit the ground.

"Good save," Gil called out automatically and caught the ball from Darby. Again, he tried to lose himself in the brilliant sunshine, the golden leaves falling around them, the feel of the mitt closing over the ball. In vain.

How am I going to get past the trial? I've got to face it and go on. I can't let it derail me. I've got to make the charges stick this time.

Gil saw himself in the courtroom that day rising as the jury had filed back in. The grim expressions on everyone's faces had signaled him that something had gone terribly wrong with his open-and-shut case.

"That's not very good," Gil's dad, whom Gil still called the Captain, yelled as he bounded down the steps of the deck to join them. "You can do better than that.'' Burly and nearly bald, the Captain took Gil's place, squatting behind Darby as catcher.

Gil shed the catcher's mitt and Darby picked up a plastic bat.

"Play ball!" the Captain ordered them.

Irritated by his father's tone, Gil lobbed the ball again.

Darby swung his bat and missed. He groaned.

"Darby, you're not trying," the Captain barked. "Keep your eye on the ball."

Darby scowled.

Gil knew how his son felt. A hung jury. A mistrial. "What a waste," he muttered, catching the ball again....

On Saturday afternoon, three days after the Putnam trial had ended in a mistrial, Patience stood in the backyard at Mrs. Honeycutt's and reached for another wooden peg in the cloth bag suspended from the clothesline. Indian summer was holding firm.

Bunny's friends, Dottie and Greta, had joined Bunny for iced tea on the front porch. Patience could hear their voices carried by the wind.

Buffeted by a warm, eager breeze, Patience was hanging her freshly laundered underclothing between lines hung with her linens. White rose-sprigged sheets fluttered around her, cooling her and bringing a fragrant clean scent of soap.

Patience liked the sense of concealment she found

in the midst of flapping damp sheets, pillowcases and towels. Ever since the moment she spoke the truth in the jury room, she'd felt exposed, worn raw by hostile glances. *Why did I give in to pique and tell them off? I could have been diplomatic.* But she'd given in to anger.

Now, daily as she walked home from school, people on the street that she didn't even know glared at her or wouldn't meet her eyes. More than once this week, she'd stepped into the teachers' lounge and been confronted by an instant silence, as though someone had flipped a switch. *Do they think I'm stupid? That I don't know they were all talking about me behind my back?*

Patience shoved a clothespin hard onto the line. *What can I do? How do I turn my situation around? I'll never be able to take a year of trouble.*

"Well, I'll be glad when this all blows over." Another snippet of the porch conversation wafted on the breeze reached her. Patience froze with her hand aiming another clothespin at the line.

"She shouldn't have let them know she was the holdout." Greta's gritty voice came on the next billow of wind. "If she hadn't owned up to it, none of them could have pointed a finger at her."

"She's an honest woman," Bunny replied.

Patience lowered her arms. *Thank you, Bunny.*

"I heard that she told them all off, called them small-town hicks." Dottie's breathy voice sounded eager with this information. "That's why that awful woman let it get out."

"You mean that Harrington woman?" Greta snapped.

"Yes, she was on the jury, too, you know." Dottie's tone oozed excitement. "And she's told everyone she ever knew—"

"That's no surprise. She's been a harpy since she was in fifth grade," Greta grumbled. "We have to think of some way to help Patience. She's a good girl, a good teacher, and she doesn't deserve the things that are being tossed around about her at the café and the Dairy Queen."

Patience hummed with sudden warmth at Greta's approval.

"Yes, I know." Bunny paused. "She's in a vulnerable position as a teacher. Parents can make trouble for her."

Bowled over by hearing this worry put into words, Patience sagged, letting her arms drop to her sides.

"The school board could refuse to offer her a second contract. She's not tenured," Greta pointed out.

"Oh, no." Dottie sounded chastened. "All this will blow over, won't it?"

I hope. Patience bent her face into the wet clothing flaring with the wind. *Lord, help me. I don't know how to turn this around...*

Halting the batting practice to give Darby some instruction, Gil positioned the small bat properly in his son's hands. "Okay, now you don't have to hit it hard, just hit it any way you can."

Facing Darby again, Gil pitched the ball low and easy.

Darby swung and missed. "Oh, man!"

"You can do better, kid," Gil's dad said in his gravelly voice. "This just takes practice." The Captain picked up the ball and lobbed it back at Gil.

"Don't expect too much of yourself at first. You'll learn. Just remember, keep your eye on the ball." Gil tossed it again.

Don't expect too much of yourself. That's what his mother had always said. Gil gave his father a narrow look. They'd lost Mom just over a year ago. His father's favorite admonition had always been the exact opposite of Gil's mother's advice. According to the Captain: Expect more of yourself or you might as well not try at all.

Gil snapped off a ball that flew past Darby and landed hard into his dad's glove.

"Hey, not so fast." The Captain gave Gil a hard look as he sent the ball back. "Give the kid a chance."

Gil tried not to frown. After retiring from the navy and then losing his wife within a year, Gil's dad had moved back to town, bought a modest home and offered to help Gil with after-school child care. All things Gil had never imagined his dad doing in a million years.

Gil tossed an easy pitch to Darby and his son managed a pop-up.

Over and over, Gil pitched, Darby swung, and the Captain caught and returned the ball. When Darby consistently failed to connect with the ball, Gil's dad grumbled loudly enough to be heard.

Gil tried to remember any time in his childhood when his dad had tried to teach him a sport. He couldn't. "Hey, you two, time for a lemonade break," Gil said, needing a break from the Captain's constant criticism of Darby.

Hot and tired of pitching, Gil headed toward the deck and kitchen.

Darby raced behind him. Soon, he grabbed a kid-size red plastic glass from his dad. "Wow, I'm thirsty."

With his thick rough fingers, Gil's dad ruffled Darby's hair. "Boys are always hungry or thirsty."

Darby gulped his lemonade and then jumped from the deck and charged the T-shaped backyard swing set. He leaped up. And with both hands, he caught the horizontal row of bars like a suspended ladder over his head and began to swing down the row, hand by hand.

"He's a regular monkey," the Captain pointed out. "I'd like to see him on an obstacle course someday."

Not dignifying this with a comment, Gil nodded

and let himself down into a lawn chair. He wiped his sweaty forehead with the hem of his T-shirt. It felt good to be out of a suit on a warm Saturday.

"Have you heard that gossip about Darby's teacher?" The Captain took a swallow from a tall, blue tumbler of lemonade.

"Where did that come from?" Gil eyed him.

"Bunny's friend, I forget her name. Don't tell me you didn't know," the Captain challenged him, "that Miss Andrews was the lone holdout on that jury?"

Of course I know. Everyone in town knows. "It doesn't matter to me who was responsible. It just means that I now have to prepare for another trial. It's a needless expense and a waste of the court's time."

"But you didn't know that Miss Andrews voted not guilty seven times?"

"Yes," he muttered, "I'd heard that."

"I thought jury deliberations were supposed to be kept confidential." The Captain let himself down onto the bench across from Gil.

"They are, but people talk. There's nothing I can do about that." But guilt snaked through him. He wasn't happy about the mistrial. He wasn't happy that Darby's teacher was being gossiped about, either. "What can I do about gossip?"

"Bunny likes her." The Captain watched intently as Darby braced his feet overhead on one bar.

"Bunny Honeycutt?" Gil asked, putting two and two together. So that's why his dad was asking about

Patience Andrews. Gil wished he had the kind of relationship where he could ask his dad if he was getting serious about Mrs. Honeycutt. But they hadn't had time to get serious, had they?

The phone rang. Empty laundry basket in her hand, Patience ran in the back door and grabbed the phone. "Hello."

"Is this Miss Andrews?" a gruff man's voice barked.

Patience hesitated and then said, "Yes, speaking."

"You think you know so much more than we do. We know all about Dan Putnam and have for years. What makes you so smart?" A string of epithets and slurs followed. And then the receiver was slammed in her ear.

Patience stood petrified with the receiver in her hand.

Bunny came up behind her and took the receiver and hung it up. "Another nasty phone call?"

Dry-mouthed, Patience nodded, trying to swallow.

"Stop answering the phone," Bunny said. "Let me get it or let it go to the answering machine."

"Why do they care so much?" Patience managed to say at last.

"People talk...unfortunately. And thin skin is a common defect that makes people nasty." Bunny squeezed her shoulder. "Now, go upstairs and try to get your mind off it. This will all blow over."

* * *

It hadn't blown over. It had only gotten worse. Now it was the week after Halloween on parents' night at Oakdale School. Patience looked out over her audience, the parents of her students. Not one smiled back at her. *Do they all hate me? Distrust me? How do I handle this, Lord?*

"The first grade is a pivotal year for your children." Patience stood tall and faced them, head-on. She tried to keep her eyes from shifting to Gil Montgomery, who lurked in the back. He sat there looking like an ad from *GQ* in contrast to the other parents, who hadn't dressed up for the evening. But his attractive outer shell wasn't what intrigued her most tonight. What was going on in his mind? Had he heard the gossip? Did he hold her responsible for his failure to convict Dan Putnam?

Her eyes strayed to him again. More importantly, had he realized what had happened to his son while she was in court? Or was he oblivious to the damage that had been done? *Lord, let me help Darby. I don't want him falling through the cracks.*

"Studies have proven that what a child experiences in the first grade can shape his whole academic future."

Gil sat on a first-grader-size chair. He pushed his feet forward and folded his arms over his chest. *That's what I'm afraid of.*

"Keeping this in mind, I am committed to helping

each of your children have a positive experience this year in my class. I don't want to do anything that will send a child down a negative path.''

Her low rich voice tantalized him like a tangible force. He felt it lowering his resistance to her. He wanted to keep his defenses up, but that voice possessed persuasive power.

''I ask that you help me in this,'' Miss Andrews continued. ''If you notice any alteration in your child's behavior at home or his or her attitude toward my class, I hope you will communicate with me as soon as possible so we can address whatever issue has developed.''

Gil shifted in his seat. *As far as I'm concerned an issue has developed over the trial and now with Darby.* Darby's teacher wore a royal-blue dress in some shiny fabric. The cloth picked up all the light in the room, making it hard not to stare at her. Why did women wear stuff like that?

''Now, some of our goals this year,'' Miss Andrews continued, ''are concrete and some are less quantifiable—''

''What does that mean?'' a man wearing a feed cap and standing behind Gil asked. The question came out as a brusque confrontation, not a polite request for information.

Miss Andrews stood her ground. ''It means that some results I can show you on paper and some will show themselves only in your children and many years in the future.''

''We know you're from Chicago,'' the man continued in a defiant tone. ''We don't want any big-city touchy-feely garbage in our school.''

Murmurs of antagonistic approval swelled around Gil.

''I really don't know what you are talking about…'' Darby's teacher dangled a piece of paper by one corner in front of her, a flimsy protective barrier.

''We don't want you experimenting with new stuff like 'new math' and 'spelling words any way you want, right or wrong' on our kids.'' A woman to Gil's right rose. ''Just teach them to read and write and do their arithmetic. That's what we're payin' you to do.''

Gil stood up. The atmosphere in the room had turned toward ugly and he couldn't permit that.

Then from the doorway behind the parents, Mrs. Canney's daunting voice issued forth. ''Miss Andrews is quite capable of teaching your children in the best possible way.''

A troubled quiet fell over the room.

''I didn't hire an unqualified teacher.'' Mrs. Canney cut them all down to size with her incisive tone. ''Miss Andrews was in the top of her class in grades and in performance in her student teaching which she did downstate, in Quincy, Illinois, *not* Chicago.''

Gil knew just how the rest of the parents felt upon

hearing the censure in Mrs. Canney's voice. He and most of them had attended Oakdale under this redoubtable principal. Mrs. Canney had just done what they had all feared as children but which had never really taken place—till now. Tonight, the principal had verbally rapped them all across the knuckles with a ruler.

"I'll leave you then, Miss Andrews," Mrs. Canney said. "Another few minutes and then I'll expect to see everyone in the cafeteria for cake and coffee."

No one responded to this, but many exchanged disgruntled glances.

Miss Andrews gazed at them, showing no weakness or concern.

Cool, calm and collected. It must be nice to have all the answers. Gil scowled at himself, at his own dissatisfaction.

"Why don't you spend the rest of the time in the room looking at the work your children have done." The teacher crumpled the paper suspended in her hands. "Some is on their desks and some is posted. I'll be at the door if you wish to speak to me further."

Gil watched the way Miss Andrews carried herself at the back of the room as she walked through the group of unsympathetic parents. She glanced neither right nor left. She showed no anxiety. She looked invincible.

Doesn't she have any weak spot, any doubt about her decisions? That must be a nice way to live.

Gil walked toward his son's desk. It dawned on him suddenly that he'd learned one thing about Miss Andrews. She possessed not only the kind of backbone that would make it possible for her to stand up to eleven other jurors and not give in, but also a roomful of hostile parents. He had to hand it to her. Like it or not, she was one gutsy lady.

Later, in the cafeteria that felt so much smaller than it had when he was a student at Oakdale, Gil watched Miss Andrews stand all alone in the crowded room, humming with conversation. No one approached her. No one glanced her way.

A shunning was taking place. Not too many miles north was an Amish settlement and Gil had heard of shunnings but he'd never witnessed one. *And we're not even Amish.*

This is Darby's teacher who spoke kindly to him after he set a squirrel rampaging through her class. Most of all, she's my son's teacher and he needs…I need her help.

Gil walked over to Miss Andrews and halted in front of her. "Good evening." He forced the words out, hoping they didn't sound as stiff as he felt.

She opened her mouth, closed it and then replied, "Good evening."

Her rich voice was even more compelling up close. "I wanted to talk to you about Darby." Gil held to his purpose.

"Yes?" Her expression gave nothing away.

''He is, I guess you could call it 'acting out' at home.'' Gil groped for words. ''He just bounces from one showdown to another with me. He can be good and then turn right around and defy me. What's his behavior like at school?''

''The same.'' She examined him as though he were an exotic display in a museum.

Why are you looking at me like that? He waited for her to go on, to tell him what he could do to stop this run of destructive misbehavior. He waited in vain.

Miss Andrews sipped the incredibly bitter coffee that he'd refused to take even one more sip of.

''What do you suggest?'' Gil pressed her.

She tightened her jaw. ''I had everything under control until I was taken away from the classroom for an extended period.''

At first, the impact of what she was saying didn't hit him. Then it did. *She's holding me responsible for Darby's misbehavior.* The sheer gall of it closed his throat to acid words that gushed up.

''I told you that day in court that I thought I would be of better use in the classroom.'' Low and fluid, her voice continued to entice him, but now heat and temper infused it. ''Why didn't you let me come back here to Darby? Everything I feared for him has happened.''

''What?'' *What had you feared? What are you talking about?*

''He didn't get along with the substitute. She concentrated on him and let him paint himself into the corner of being the class behavior problem. *That* was exactly what I was trying to prevent, but it all happened that ten days I was away from him.''

The accusations came one after the other, allowing him no time to respond.

''And now you're probably mad at me, too, because I voted not guilty.'' The lady glared at him, her jaw moving as though she were chewing nails. Stale ones.

''I didn't bring that up—''

''Oh, really? Your eyes did. They are extremely eloquent. When you walked into my classroom tonight, you looked ready and willing to strangle me.''

''Looks can't kill.'' Gil took a step closer to her. Her fragrance enveloped him, flowers and sunshine.

''But they can wound.'' Her voice continued to rise. ''And I'm tired of being the target of everyone's animosity. Dan Putnam was not proven guilty of attacking his mother—''

Her words ripped off the last layer of his restraint. ''Yes, he was. My case convinced eleven out of twelve jurors. I prosecuted the right man. Solving crimes isn't like those TV shows where they make up forensic evidence that doesn't exist in the real world. You just think you know more than the rest of us…hicks.''

''That's not true.'' She leaned even closer.

His pulse spiked. Was it due to their argument or

just her, just the way her eyes flashed and her presence had defied him?

"This has nothing to do with my being from Chicago. It has everything to do with small-minded prejudice and prejudging people with mental illness. I happened to know that that happens even in big cities."

"I prosecuted the right man." Gil wanted to shout at her, rail at her, but he stuck to the plain truth.

"Then start a new investigation that actually provides some evidence to convict Dan Putnam of being guilty of something more than shouting and arguing with his mother. I dare you to find any real, hard evidence that would convict him. Your case had no evidence. You just relied on his history of mental illness and thought that would be enough to convict him."

"Many cases in the real world suffer from a lack of hard evidence. My case didn't depend on Putnam's history but on motive and opportunity."

"You never even looked for anyone else with motive and opportunity, much less evidence."

"Well, I'm going to have to come up with new evidence. Because of you, I have to retry the case. And this time, Dan Putnam will be convicted."

"Probably." She cast him a look of pure disdain. "But will the real culprit be convicted? I don't think so."

Chapter Four

Later, under the clear and starry November sky, Patience dragged herself home from parents' night. The street was silent except for her own footsteps and the wind shaking bare tree branches overhead. The stark and lonely sound echoed through her. The leaves had all fallen and so had her hopes.

This is not going to blow over. The rest of the school year, I'll be the targeted teacher. And when it comes time to renew my contract, I'll get a "Please don't call us, we'll call you" letter instead.

Tears smarted in her eyes. *Lord, you know how happy I was that you provided me with this job. Why can't anyone see that I was only acting on my conscience when I voted not guilty? Why did Gil Montgomery take it personally when it wasn't? And why did I let my anger burst out again? Why can't I keep my cool about this?*

Thinking of the father made her think of his son. *And you know how much I wanted to do for Darby. It's all gone now, exploded in my face. But Darby will suffer the most.*

How can I turn this around for that little boy? I don't want him to go through the rest of his school years as "that Montgomery kid." I already hear that tone in other teachers' voices when they monitor him on the playground or in the cafeteria. It isn't right. He didn't deserve this. Why can't anyone see how he's crying out for love?

What a horrible night, Lord. She walked up the sidewalk to Mrs. Honeycutt's house, her safe haven. Once inside, she could lay down her sword and shield and relax. That's all she wanted now. Lights glimmered in the high, wide windows, and a cheery welcome would be on Bunny's lips. *Thank you, Lord, I have at least one friend here.*

The door opened and Bunny motioned her in. "You have company, dear." She stepped aside to reveal a painfully thin woman standing with drooping shoulders in the parlor arch.

Patience gasped. A moment of stunned silence and then anger—a blazing heat—surged through her.

"Patience…" The woman's voice was rough from years of smoking and vodka. "Hello."

"Mother?" Patience tried to think of something more to say. But she couldn't. Stalling for time, she took off her coat and hung it on the hall tree by the door, trying to think of words, any words polite enough that she could voice in front of Bunny. Patience turned back and faced her mother.

"I know I've surprised you." Her mother looked at her, pleading with her for...what?

Did she want Patience to act like a daughter happy to see a beloved mother? The thought galled Patience, almost gagging her.

She tightened her self-control. "That's right. I didn't expect you, Mother." The clipped words were the right ones for this situation, but she hadn't been able to make them sound completely natural. *This is all I need—on top of everything else.*

Bunny's eyebrows lifted. "I was just going to make us a pot of herbal tea. I'll go do that while you two chat." She waved them toward the parlor where a small fire burned on the grate.

Patience obeyed her landlady and moved into the room decorated with comfortable floral-print furniture and sat down by the cozy hearth. Her mother sat down in the wing-back chair across from hers. The crackling of the pine fire was the only sound in the room. Patience banked down the inner flames that had consumed her at seeing her mother here tonight.

Her mother picked at her ragged nails and stared downward.

"Why are you here?" Patience asked finally.

"Did Mike..." Her mother dabbed at her eyes with

a tissue from her jeans' pocket. "Did he tell you what happened to me while you were still in school?"

Patience stared into the flickering fire. "Yes, he did. When did they let you out of jail?"

Her mother let out a gasping sort of sob. "Just a few days ago."

The wounded sound bothered Patience, but she steeled herself against it. *No one asked you here and I know your tricks too well.*

"Then let me guess," Patience pressed on. "You needed a place to stay and no one else would take you in." The coldness in Patience's own voice shocked her. How could she burn inside with fury yet speak with frigid politeness?

"Patience, please, that's not why I've come—"

"I only want to know when you'll be leaving."

Her mother sobbed again. "Don't, Patience. Please don't be cruel."

"Why? *Because you're my mother?*" Her words, steeped in caustic sarcasm, oozed up from a deep dark sore spot inside Patience.

Bunny bustled in. "Such a chilly night. Winter is just around the corner."

Patience watched her friend set down a tray and begin pouring and serving tea. Patience accepted hers but had no inclination to lift the cup to her lips, her numb lips. Jonesy ambled into the room and brushed Patience's ankles.

I'm numb all over. Lord, why is she here? Wasn't everything bad enough as it was?

"Now, Mrs. Andrews," Bunny began.

"She doesn't have the same last name as I do," Patience said, again in a harsh voice she barely recognized as her own. "Her name is Scudder."

"Yes," her mom said, holding her china cup. "But please call me Martina."

Bunny stared at Patience but addressed her mother. "I'm afraid it slipped my mind. I'm Bunny. Patience, I told your mother what a difficult time you've been having."

"You did?" Patience lifted the cup to her lips and forced in a sip of warm liquid. *You should have saved your breath, Bunny.*

"Yes, I thought she should know what you're up against and I thought it would be easier on you if I explained it all to her."

Yes, I do have a friend in you, Bunny. "Thanks."

"How did tonight go?" Bunny asked. "Did you make any headway?"

"No." Patience felt the sudden and overwhelming urge to pour out everything, even in her mother's presence. "My students' parents gave a good impression of a lynch mob. With Gil Montgomery in the lead, carrying a rope."

"No." Martina looked shocked.

Yes, this isn't about you, Mother, like you think everything is. "The worst part came in the cafeteria during the coffee time. Gil came over to talk to me about Darby and I'm afraid I lost it.''

''What did you say?'' Bunny got up, moved the fire screen and stirred the fire.

''I reminded him that when I had appeared in court, I told him I thought I'd be of more use in the classroom than on a jury.''

''I bet he didn't like that.'' Bunny put the blackened fire screen back into place and sat down beside Patience.

Patience hmmphed. ''You better believe he didn't. I told him that Darby didn't get along with my substitute and then she helped Darby brand himself as a behavior problem—exactly what I was trying to prevent.''

Martina looked confused, but Patience ignored this. Her mother never cared about what happened in her daughter's life anyway. That would never change.

''What did Gil say to that?'' Bunny lifted her own cup. The mantel clock chimed ten times.

''Nothing. He knows something's gone wrong with his son, but he doesn't know how it came about or what to do.''

''Did he mention the trial?'' Bunny didn't take her eyes off Patience.

Her concern bathed Patience like a soothing cream over her jagged nerves. ''Yes, I told him that he'd relied on Dan Putnam's history of mental illness, assumed that explained the attack on Mrs. Perkins and hadn't really investigated at all.''

Bunny pursed her lips.

Profound fatigue rolled over Patience. ''What does it matter what I said to him? Everyone there tonight except for Mrs. Canney has branded me 'a behavior problem,' too. Darby and I will be *persona non grata* for the rest of the year. And in the spring, my contract won't be renewed and that's that.'' Patience lifted her cup and swallowed a mouthful of fragrant cinnamon-flavored tea, letting it soothe her tight throat.

''You mustn't say that,'' Bunny scolded. ''You can turn this around.''

''How?'' Patience asked.

''Well, personally, I think that neighbor, Fiskus, had more motive than Dan. We've got to do some digging ourselves, I guess.'' Bunny sounded encouraging. ''I mean, if Gil Montgomery has his mind made up, he won't be looking for evidence to acquit. I bet if you found just one fact he hadn't come across, you could get him to listen to you.''

Patience held her cup in front of her mouth, considering this. ''You might have something there.''

Martina shrugged. ''Men never think women know anything.''

For once, Patience had to agree with her mother.

''Too true.'' Bunny grinned. ''Patience, I told your mother she can stay in my guest room until she finds a place of her own.''

"A place of her own?" Patience's fingers congealed around her cup. "I thought you just came for a short visit, *Mother*." She couldn't help twisting the word *mother*.

"No, after your stepfather's death, I decided to make a fresh start here in Rushton. I wanted to be near you."

Patience stared at her mother. *This is all I needed to make my life perfect. A perfect hell.*

On Saturday morning, Patience walked into the entrance of the Rose Care Center, a newer one-story retirement home. Though her nerves vibrated, she made herself walk nonchalantly to the information desk. "Hi, I'm new in the area and I was wondering if the care center has a volunteer organization."

A young girl in jeans and a white sweatshirt with royal-blue lettering—At Rose We Care—looked up. "Yes, we do. Would you like to volunteer?"

Patience nodded. *I want to volunteer, but I also want to find out all I can about Mrs. Perkins.*

"Would you fill out this form?" The teen offered her a clipboard and pen.

Patience filled in the blanks on the five-by-six card asking for name, address, and such and handed it back.

"Mrs. Grantley is the head of our volunteers. She will be in shortly."

"May I just look around while I wait?" Patience

glanced around the well-decorated lobby with many luxuriant green rubber plants and hanging Boston ferns.

"Sure."

"Thank you." Patience relaxed the tiniest bit as she followed the hall to the right. The name of each resident was posted right beneath the room number beside each door. *Very convenient for finding someone. Mrs. Perkins, where are you?*

An inner voice parried, *"But the woman can't talk. What do you expect to find out?"*

I don't know. But I have to start somewhere.

"You think—" the voice didn't give up *"—you're going to be able to find out more than the sheriff and the D.A.?"*

Give me a break. Maybe I won't find anything, but I have to start looking. This case has forced me into a tight corner. If I don't take action, I'll be looking for a new job next summer and how will that look on applications? A teacher should last longer than one year at a school district.

And Bunny's right. I have to try to dig myself out of this. If Mrs. Perkins can't talk today, what about tomorrow? If I volunteer here, at least I'll know if and when Mrs. Perkins regains her faculties.

Then, there she stood, at Mrs. Perkins's door, room 103. Patience hesitated on the threshold of the semi-private room. Which of the two ladies in the two beds was Mrs. Perkins?

"Hi." A gray-haired woman sitting beside one of the two residents in room 103 looked up.

"Hi." Patience stepped into the room. "I'm just looking around. I've just signed up as a volunteer here."

"Oh?" The woman looked surprised.

"How long has—" Patience nodded toward the woman in the bed "—been a resident here?"

"Bertha's been here just a few months."

Ah, so this was Bertha Perkins. "How pleased are you with the accommodations here?" Patience tried to sound politely disinterested.

"Why do you ask?" The woman sounded suspicious.

"Because I don't want to volunteer somewhere that isn't doing a good job." Patience walked to the end of Mrs. Perkins's bed and gazed at the plump woman who was in turn studying her. The eyes behind the glasses looked intelligent and alert, but Patience noted that one arm lay helpless at her side.

"Ah." Mrs. Perkins's visitor nodded. "Well, this is only the second time I've been here. I live out of town. I'm Phyllis, Bertha's sister-in-law from her second marriage."

"Hi, I'm Patience." She shook the woman's dry crepe-paper hand and sat down in a chair beside her.

"This place seems okay," the sister-in-law continued, still holding the magazine she'd been reading. "Bertha's been getting physical therapy every other day. I'm hopin' she'll be able to get out of her bed and back home sometime soon. I keep talkin' to her, hopin' she'll try to talk back to me. But so far, not a word.''

"Did she have a stroke?" Patience asked, hoping to get more information as she returned Mrs. Perkins's examination of her.

"Yes, it's awful. Her home was robbed and she was attacked.'' The woman leaned closer. "It was her own son that did it.''

"Really?'' Patience affected surprise. Her heart plummeted.

"Yeah, that boy always was a problem to her. Everybody knows that. I told her when he come back to town a year ago. I said, 'Bertha, that boy wants somethin'. You make sure he don't talk you outta your house, talk you into a nursin' home or somethin'.'''

Patience nodded and tried to look sympathetic.

"I never thought to warn her about him attacking her. But I shoulda known. He's been in mental hospitals. You never know with them kind of people, do you? And now Bertha's laid up here and what's going to happen to her? There's only me and that boy of hers and he's in jail.''

"Oh, there you are.'' The teen from the information desk paused in the doorway. "Miss Andrews, Mrs. Grantley will see you now.''

Patience rose, the sister-in-law's words revolving in her mind. "Goodbye. It's been nice talking to you.''

She turned to the woman in the bed. Mrs. Perkins, maybe I'll drop in and see you again.'' Patience walked out. *What a shame. Even Bertha's sister-in-law thinks it was Dan.*

''I needed to find a job and I can't drive with a suspended license.'' Patience's mother would not meet her daughter's eyes. She talked to the tabletop in the tiny kitchen upstairs in Patience's apartment. Several days had passed since Martina's appearing in Rushton. ''I saw the ad in the newspaper and thought it was something I could do. So I called and went over to talk to the woman.''

''Mother, most people don't work here in Rushton.'' Patience sat across from her at the small table. ''They work at the packing plant in the next town or at the mall in Marion.''

Her mother made no reply.

Patience cast around trying to come up with a way to discourage her mother from getting settled in here. ''I rented this apartment because I can walk to the downtown stores and to school. I don't want the expense of a car this year. I'm trying to pay off my school loans as quickly as I can.''

''I'm sorry I wasn't able to help pay for your education.'' Her mother stared at her lap.

Patience stopped herself from making a comment about the high price tag on vodka. Why dredge up the past? What good would it do? And why try to fight her mother on this idea of getting a job? It wouldn't work out. But let her mother find that out for herself.

"Well, I need to make some income and neither of us is driving," her mother repeated. "That's why I thought selling cosmetics door to door might be a good idea for me."

A thought about the investigation started in Patience's mind. Would that work?

"I've found out where the local AA meetings take place. I'm going to go tomorrow. It's at the red brick church on the square. I can walk there. Would you like to come with me?" Martina hazarded a glance at Patience.

"Mother, I'm already in trouble with the local population. What would they think if I showed up in an AA meeting on the town square?"

"I'm sorry. I didn't think." Martina concentrated on her lap again.

Her mother's beaten-down quality was wearing thin on Patience. AA notwithstanding, she couldn't believe Martina wouldn't start drinking again. Then there would be embarrassing and frustrating scenes where her mother would try to justify her erratic and self-destructive behavior, blaming it all on Patience. When that didn't work, then she'd blow up and leave town. This had happened so many times. Patience could have written the script herself.

Then that thought about the case popped up again and Patience recalled Bertha Perkins's address, Walnut Street, which was an easy walking distance from here. *The neighbors had heard the argument between Dan and his mother. But maybe they had information that the police had ignored or the D.A. hadn't bothered to present in his case.* "Well, if you're determined, I might go around with you, dropping off brochures."

"That would be nice." Her mother beamed. "How about this afternoon after school? We can hand out the brochures and introduce ourselves."

Patience nodded. *And if we go down Walnut Street, maybe someone will have something to say about the attack on Bertha Perkins. Events have proven that in this gossipy town, it won't be hard to get people talking about it.*

In the thin late-afternoon light two days before Thanksgiving, Patience looked up from her desk. Gil Montgomery—in an expensive khaki trench coat that made his hair look darker—stood in her classroom doorway. How could her spirits rise and fall in a split second? "Hello."

"Good afternoon." He entered and approached her desk.

Her senses went on high alert. Patience's world was populated by kids and other women. Even the janitor at Oakdale was female. That must be what made her extra susceptible to men. Especially this man. Why did he have to look so good? "What can I do for you, Mr. Montgomery?"

In front of her desk, he stood looking down at her.

Was he finally here to ask advice on how to handle Darby? She refused to show any of her reaction to his presence or to rise to the bait. Let him make the first comment.

Gil knew what he wanted to say to this woman, staring up at him with her large brown eyes, brooding eyes. He needed her help and he needed her cooperation. Would he be able to get both or either? Their clash at parents' night almost three weeks ago still left a bad taste in his mouth and he didn't doubt she felt the same wariness. "May I sit down?"

She barely nodded toward an adult-size chair at the side of the room.

Her stiff reception only made him more determined. He dragged it over and sat down.

They stared at each other for several long moments.

"I'm sorry that you have forced me to come and speak to you." Gil's face froze in a grim expression that he wouldn't soften.

She raised one cocky, perfect golden eyebrow.

"It's come to my attention that you have been visiting Mrs. Perkins at the care center." His jaw ached with tension.

"I volunteer at the care center." She didn't even look at him, but continued marking a student's homework paper. "I visit several people while I'm there."

"Yes, but what caused you to volunteer there?" *How stupid do you think I am?*

She shrugged her slender shoulders. "Aren't I free to volunteer wherever I want?"

"If your only goal is to volunteer—" he let his outrage seep into his tone "—and *not* to interfere with my investigation into a case."

She folded her long graceful arms over each other, still holding a red pencil. "I'm just being a good citizen."

He was struck by this woman's cool, self-contained quality. It contrasted so with the casual, easy way his ex-wife had about her. "And is good citizenship the reason why you have been prowling around Mrs. Perkins' neighborhood asking questions?"

"I have not been prowling around anywhere." She tapped the desk top with the metal end of the red pencil. "I've been helping my mother hand out brochures. She's selling cosmetics door to door."

"Your mother?" No one had mentioned a mother to him. "Why is she here?"

"Maybe you should ask my mother." Patience's soft-looking lips thinned. "But certainly she has a right to make a living."

"Why do I get the feeling you aren't being candid with me?" He leaned his elbows on the front edge of her desk, refusing to lower his guard. Even as it irritated him, her refusal to give in attracted him. Miss

Patience Andrews would never take the path of least resistance.

"The trial is over." She pushed back her chair a few inches—away from him. "I'm not on your jury. The only topic we now have in common is your son. Do you want to discuss him? If not, I have work to do."

He stared at her. "I'm not surprised, Miss Andrews, that you aren't willing to talk to me about what you are up to. But I don't want you messing around and ruining a second trial."

"How could I do that?" Her eyes flickered over him and then dropped to the paper in front of her.

"By stirring up rumors—" he watched her, trying to guess what she would parry with "—and muddying testimony from people who may be called on to testify."

"Mrs. Perkins is still unable to speak and probably won't be able to testify any time soon. If the neighbors are that easy to sway, maybe their testimony wasn't worth much to begin with." Patience picked up another student paper and began reading it.

Don't try to dismiss me. I'm not done with you. "I received calls about your *visits* to Mrs. Perkins's neighbors. I've let them know that they can take legal action if you continue to harass them."

Patience glared at him over the sheet of paper. "If they don't want to order cosmetics, no one's forcing them to. Did you have any questions for me about

Darby now? Or perhaps I may take legal action because you are harassing me.''

''Why are you meddling?'' Not an inch. She wouldn't give an inch.

''I'm not meddling. I'm just trying to win back my reputation. Maybe you enjoy people gossiping about you, speaking ill of you. But I don't. Don't you realize the spot you've put me into—just because you insisted I neglect your son and take part on the jury? How much clearer could I have made it to you that day you questioned me in court?''

He stared at her. Her full lower lip pouted, snagging his attention. He wet his lips. ''*My* only concern is that justice be done.''

''*My* only concern is that justice be done,'' she repeated, pinning him back with her gaze. ''And not only to Dan Putnam, but to me. What have you done about trying to come up with some hard evidence? Or are you still sure that Dan will be prosecuted just because I won't be on the jury this time?''

He glared at her.

''Now do you want to discuss your son? And let me say, we need to discuss him. He's in a dreadful state of turmoil. Have you and your ex-wife been in conflict lately?''

''I hardly think that is any of your business,'' Gil snapped.

''It is when it affects the way Darby behaves in

class. The child needs calm in his life, not emotional scenes. Do you realize that?''

He stared at her, wishing she didn't sound so right.

''If you're not ready to discuss Darby—'' she dismissed him with her eyes ''—please leave. I have work to do.''

''I'm warning—'' Gil's cell phone rang. ''Hello.''

''Gil, Coreena wouldn't listen to me.'' Bunny's voice came out strained and breathless.

''What?'' He stood, shoving the chair back.

''The Captain had to take care of something in Marion, so I came to his place to watch Darby after school. Coreena stopped by with that new boyfriend of hers…'' Bunny paused and he could sense her swallowing a criticism of his ex-wife's choice in men. ''Anyway, he has a Harley and they wanted to take Darby with them for a ride. I tried to tell them that his bike helmet wasn't adequate for use on a motorcycle, but off they went. I just wish the Captain had been here. Do you think they somehow knew he wasn't?''

Gil felt like cursing. ''I'll be right home.''

Chapter Five

A frosty November wind blowing down the neck of his jacket, Gil paced the deck overlooking his backyard. He'd decided to wait here rather than at his mother's. Coreena would bring Darby back here since she'd expect Gil to be home by now. He checked his watch again. Nearly seven o'clock. *Lord, help me handle this with calmness, not anger. Darby is the important one here. Miss Andrews got that much through to me today.*

His agitation had forced him out of his warm kitchen into the chilly afternoon. He shoved his ungloved fists into his pockets and headed down the length of the deck one more time.

He cracked his knuckles savagely. *I can't blame anybody else. The worst mistake of my life was marrying that woman. Why couldn't I really see her, see that her careless ways wouldn't fit mine? But I can't let Darby continue to pay the price for my lack of judgment.*

From the alley, the rumble of a motorcycle halted him in his tracks. He turned and watched as Coreena, her boyfriend and Darby pulled in the drive at the rear of the lot.

Dressed all in black leather, Coreena slid off the cycle from behind her boyfriend. With a flourish, she swung off her helmet and helped Darby down from the circle of the boyfriend's arms. She took Darby's hand and sauntered through the back gate and into the yard with an exaggerated feminine swing to her body. *You're not trying to get my attention with that, Coreena. That's for your new boyfriend.*

Pink-faced from the cold, Darby bounced at her side. "Dad! Dad! I got to ride on Blaine's Harley. It's so cool." His boy charged up the steps to Gil and wrapped his small arms around Gil's thighs.

Gil sucked in the angry words that had been roiling through his mind for the past hour and patted his son on the head. "That sounds exciting, son." The approving words chafed his throat.

"It was great." Giving a jump, Darby pumped his hand in the air and then pivoted toward the burly man still straddling his bike. Darby waved. "Thanks again, Blaine!"

"No problem, munchkin." The large man's gruff

voice rumbled over the yard, like a warning, a challenge.

Miss Andrews's words, "Darby needs calm in his life," replaying in his mind, Gil pushed down his churning outrage. *How did the teacher know we've enacted too many emotional scenes in front of Darby? Way too many.*

Gil carefully chose a neutral tone of voice. "Coreena, if you're going to take Darby on that...motorcycle again, he'll need a motorcycle helmet." Wintry wind gusted around them, billowing Coreena's big hair.

"I'm kind of short of cash right now." She brushed strands away from her mouth. "These leathers cost me a bundle." Acting impervious to the elements, she lounged against the deck railing, taunting him, confident that she still could turn any man's head.

But not mine. Not ever again. "I'll buy the helmet." Gil made himself focus on her conniving eyes. In a flash, again he saw Patience Andrews, so genuine and earnest, sitting at her desk, a red pencil in her hand. What a contrast. "Just make sure *in the future* that our son has it on when he's on that...bike."

"Okay. Blaine was really careful today. He doesn't want anything to happen to my kid, you know." She swung around, flipping her mane of gold-and-brown hair toward him, and danced down the steps.

"I'm glad to hear that." Gil stared after her. He

finally admitted to himself that all those years ago, her attraction had been mainly physical.

"Hey, Dad," Darby called from the back door. "Can we have hot dogs for supper?"

Gil nodded. *At least* I'm *the only one too upset to eat.* Gil wished that Patience Andrews had been here to see the harm her words had prevented. He owed her thanks for avoiding another destructive scene. *I need help understanding my son, Lord. But I'm only human and I wish I didn't have to take it from that woman.*

Thanksgiving Day at Bunny's should have been pleasant for Patience. She sincerely liked her landlady. And in spite of everything, she'd looked forward to the start of the holiday season. But that was before Bunny had informed her, on Thanksgiving morning, that in addition to Dottie, she'd invited Gil's father, Captain Montgomery, Darby and Gil.

Gil Montgomery. Why did he have to be here? And why had Bunny placed them right next to each other? Every time Patience looked up, she sensed Gil's blue eyes studying her profile.

Gil tried not to stare at Patience. *Why does she have to look so good?*

Darby's teacher wore a soft golden-yellow cashmere sweater and a matching wool skirt. A string of pearls and matching earrings gave her a delicate fairy-tale-princess look.

"This is good turkey," Darby announced.

"Thank you." Bunny smiled at Darby and then the Captain. "You be sure to eat enough. This is the first year in a long time that I was able to buy a really big one."

"How big?" his son asked from his place on the other side of Patience.

"Twenty-five pounds of bird."

"Wow." Darby sounded awed.

"It's wonderful." The frail woman who'd been introduced to Gil as Martina, Patience's mother, looked up for a fraction of a second and then back down at her plate.

Gil had tried to put Patience and her mother together, but they didn't look anything alike. Martina wore a shabby sweater, a man's shirt and blue jeans. Patience's complexion was peaches and cream, a phrase he recalled his mother using to describe a girl he'd once dated. In contrast, Martina was sallow and drawn.

Maybe he wasn't the only one who didn't look anything like his child.

Patience's linen napkin slid off her lap.

Gil bent to retrieve it at the same moment Patience did.

Their heads nearly brushed each other. "Stop staring at me," she whispered in an irritated tone. "And eat your dinner."

His face burned. *I don't like this woman.* He straightened up. *But I can't take my eyes off her.*

"Darby, I think you should move your milk glass up a little," Patience murmured. "You don't want to bump it with your arm."

The words were barely out of the woman's mouth, when Darby reached for the glass and managed to spill it.

Patience leaped up as milk flowed over her skirt.

"Darby!" the Captain bellowed.

"Don't yell at him," Gil snapped. "It's just an accident."

Crestfallen, Darby jumped up and ran through the door to the kitchen. Patience hurried after him.

Wanting to follow but forced to use several napkins tossed to him by the other diners, Gil staunched the flow of milk.

"Captain, Gil's right," Bunny said. "It's just an accident. My linens are all washable. No big deal."

The Captain's face had reddened with embarrassment.

He's my son, Dad, so you don't have to be embarrassed. Darby's behavior is my responsibility. And Bunny sounded sincere. She wasn't upset over the episode.

"Gil," Bunny said, "why don't you go out to the kitchen and bring back some moist and some dry paper towels. We'll clean up this mess in no time."

Gil nodded and left carrying the milk-soaked linen. He found Patience sitting in a kitchen chair with

Darby standing in front of her. She was talking softly to his son. "Now here's your dad. I bet you anything he isn't mad at you. Accidents happen." She implored Gil with a glance.

He read the request and made his voice light. Her concern for his son touched him, but at the same time, her assumption that he'd come out to scold Darby griped him. "That's right. No harm done."

He tossed the wet napkins into the sink and went to wash his hands. "Mrs. Honeycutt just wants us to bring out some wet and some dry paper towels. We'll have this cleaned up in a jiffy."

"Really?" Darby leaned against Patience's shoulder.

"Really." Gil dried his hands with a paper towel from the holder next to the sink. "Now let's go out and clean up the spill and then we can get back to that twenty-five-pound turkey."

Finally, Darby grinned and accepted a bunch of dry paper towels from Gil.

"I'll just slip upstairs and put on slacks," Patience said and walked through the door to the hall.

Gil watched her go. The milk had probably ruined an expensive skirt, but she'd still spoken gently to his son. This made the decision for him. "Now I know what I have to do."

Patience held the receiver to her ear and listened as it rang. The day after Thanksgiving and several days after Gil had stopped by to lecture Patience in her room at school, fluffy featherlike snow floated outside her bedroom window. His visit lingered in her mind—how handsome he'd looked and how irritating his voice had been. An unpleasant mix. *Then why don't you just put him out of your mind?*

The line picked up and she pushed Gil out of her thoughts. "Hello, is this Mr. Pulaski?" Patience fiddled with the telephone cord as she sat on her faded blue quilt-covered bed. Would this phone call get her the help she needed? Would a retired Chicago cop still have an "in" with his department?

"Yes?" the gruff voice answered her. "I already have a long-distance company and I don't want to buy anything—"

"This is Patience Andrews, Gracie's cousin," she cut in. "Do you remember me?"

"Let me see." Silence. "Oh, I know. You're that pretty blonde who worked for Jack this summer at his office. What can I do for you?"

She grinned at his lightly sexist compliment. "Well, it's a little hard to explain. I hope you don't think I'm being presumptuous, but I was talking to Gracie and she said you were the person to call."

"I love that Gracie." Mr. Pulaski's voice warmed.

Patience smiled, thinking of her petite and dynamic cousin. "We all do."

"Now what can I do for you, miss?"

"I'm down here in Rushton." Her mind went over what she'd prepared to say to him. *Will he think I'm paranoid or just plain nuts?* "I'm just starting my first year as a teacher."

"Yes."

"And I was chosen for jury duty in October."

"What kind of case?" Curiosity sparked in the man's voice.

"An assault and robbery. Anyway, I didn't think the local D.A. presented a very solid case. Primarily, it was just circumstantial evidence propped up by the fact that the suspect had a history of mental illness."

"Ah." He sounded interested.

"I was wondering if you could advise me." Patience took the plunge. "You see, I was the one responsible for the hung jury and it's a small town. Everyone is down on me—"

"That information should have been kept confidential," Mr. Pulaski growled.

"It should have been, but some other jurors let it be known that my vote was the only not guilty. And my reputation has taken a beating. And this being my first year teaching here, I want to do something to clear myself of being a know-it-all crackpot."

He chuckled. "How can I help you, little lady?"

"The items stolen were antiques, family heirlooms. Some were quite valuable. I was thinking that some might make their way to Chicago, maybe to antique dealers there."

"Ah. I see." He paused. "Yes, you're probably right. Some might have headed south to Nashville, too. That's a popular antiques town."

Great. He's taking me seriously. "You sound like you know what you're talking about, Mr. Pulaski."

"Antiques aren't a popular theft item, but it does happen. Let me guess. You'd like me to ask some of my friends on the force to keep an eye out for some of the items?"

"Yes, that's it." Cool relief whistled through her. "I thought if they turn up for sale in Chicago, it would mean that the local man couldn't have done it. He was arrested almost immediately after the attack."

"That might be right. Unless he had already hooked up with someone in his area that had connections. Are there any antique stores in the area?"

"A few." She pictured the town square and its few quaint shops.

"You should check them out. See if any of them have a criminal record."

"How would I do that?" she asked.

"The easiest way is to use small-town gossip to your advantage. Ask around. If a dealer has been around for several years, people usually can tell you if he's on the up-and-up or not."

"I see. I'll do that." The afternoon gossip group that had moved into Bunny's living room because of the chillier temperatures would be meeting soon and she'd be there with a few prepared questions. "Also, could you look up three names? I know one of them has a criminal record but the others might have something in their past also.''

''What are the names?'' Mr. Pulaski asked.

''Wade Bevin, Cal Fiskus and Hank Drulow.'' She spelled each name for him.

''Okay, got 'em. Now—'' Mr. Pulaski's voice became businesslike ''—if you get me descriptions of the stuff, I'll hand it off to friends of mine who are still on the force and maybe they will even contact Nashville and a few other hot antiques towns.''

''Oh, Mr. Pulaski, that would be wonderful. Thank you.''

''The people down there giving you a lot of grief about this, huh?'' he said as though trying to find a way to offer her sympathy.

''It's been tense.'' Patience shuddered, remembering the cold looks she still got when walking around the town square.

''You're too pretty a girl and too nice for that kind of stuff.'' The man's voice became bluff and reassuring. ''Leave it to me. I'll do what I can.''

''Thank you so much. I really appreciate this. You just don't know how much.'' She took a breath. ''I'll e-mail the information to Gracie and Jack and they'll bring it over to you.''

''That'll work. Now don't you worry. You're not in this alone.''

Feeling weak with sudden relief, Patience hung up

the phone and then flopped back on her soft quilt with a sigh.

The phone rang. She glanced at it and ignored it, letting the message go to the machine.

"Hello, Miss Andrews, this is Gil. I would like to set up a meeting with you about my son. Please call me at my office so we can set up a time. Thank you."

Waves of sensation and confused emotions lapping inside, Patience stared at the phone. Gil's deep voice had held a quality so different, so much different from the tone she'd heard from him when he'd come to school. This time, the man had sounded sincere and…meek…almost. Could that be possible?

On Saturday morning after Thanksgiving, Patience nudged the cart down the aisle of the local grocery store. Inside her, a battle waged. Trying to concentrate on the grocery list was not keeping her mind in order. Willfully, Gil Montgomery's deep voice and dark chocolate-brown hair kept intruding.

Her mother trailed beside her. "If we buy the large size of vegetable oil, it will cost less."

"Yes, but we have to carry the groceries home ourselves," Patience reminded her. "And how long would it take us to use up the economy size?"

"You're right," her mother agreed in a flat voice.

Gil's phone call played in her mind again. Patience pushed the call out of her mind and tried instead, to think kind thoughts about this thin, pale woman beside her.

But it's so hard, Lord. I feel such resentment toward my mother. I don't want to feel it. I know it's against your will, but I'm struggling. And it doesn't help when I expect her to slide back to her old self at any moment. She's tried to dry out before....

"Hello."

Gil's voice from just behind made her stop her cart and look up. Warmth she had no control over rushed through her whole body. Was it attraction or embarrassment?

"I wonder if you got my call the other night," he asked.

"Yes, I've...I've been very busy." Patience voiced a convenient alibi. She cleared her throat.

Irritated with her pat excuse, Gil nodded and tried to make his voice more engaging. He hated having to make this effort, but it had to be done. What was good for his son was more important than how much this schoolteacher annoyed him. He eyed the silent woman beside Patience "Hello, Mrs. Scudder."

Patience's mother nodded and stared at the linoleum.

Well, he obvious didn't impress her much. He turned to Patience, fortifying himself against her inexplicable appeal. *So what do you want me to say, Patience? In light of our conflict over the case, what do I have to do to get your cooperation and input on helping Darby?*

"You wanted to get together and discuss your son," Patience prompted him in that low voice of hers that made his nerves hum.

"Yes, when would it be convenient?"

She glanced away from him, not meeting his gaze. "How about after school on Monday?"

He rested his hand next to hers on the shopping-cart handle. "Monday might work out, but I was wondering if you'd meet me in the evening?"

"Evening?" She gave him a startled look as if he'd proposed something improper. "Why?"

"Because I often can't get to school while you are still there." He moved his hand nearer to hers as if closing in on her. *Because I'm hoping if I am seen with you in public, it will show that I've overlooked your role in the Putnam mistrial. Then I hope the controversy will die down and you won't have to meddle in my affairs any further. And then we can concentrate on Darby.*

Waiting for her reply, he paused to let his gaze soak in her elegant figure and to note her complete lack of flirtation. Patience always filled him with conflicting emotions and he seemed to affect her the same way. It was hard not to like this honest woman. *And I'd like to see you away from school in the evening because for once, I'd like you not to be irritated with me when we talk.*

"Where would we meet?" she asked, making direct eye contact. "Your office?"

"No, how about the café on the square?" *I want as many people as possible to see us together.*

"When?"

He decided suddenly to push harder. Why did she push back? Why did she always fence with him? "How about I pick you up at seven tonight?"

"Tonight? You suggested Monday." She stared at him with her large fawn-brown eyes.

"Why put it off?" His own unexpected switch in tactics made his blood pump. Time to shake this woman up, stop her from meddling and get her back on Darby, her real job. "Why not tonight? Why don't I take you to supper?"

Chapter Six

At the rear of the Corner Café, Patience stared across the booth at Gil. In contrast to the dark November night, the café sparkled so clean and bright. Too bright. When they had walked in *together,* the bustling Saturday-night café had fallen silent.

Patience's face still flamed with embarrassment. Hot currents of frustration and outrage roiled inside her. "I told you this was a mistake." *Why did I let you persuade me to come here? With* you *of all people?*

From behind the vinyl-covered menu, Gil muttered, "And I said, *for once,* have some faith in my judgment. If we're seen together, not arguing, the gossip about our feud will start dropping off the chart. I'm trying to help you."

She lifted her menu, but the printed list of entrées

squiggled in front of her eyes. "I don't think this is going to help," she muttered back at him.

"So much for 'trust me.'" Gil sounded grim.

Patience was struck by his tone. She looked at him and found herself fascinated by the cleft in his square chin. Did it point to a gentleness that belied the hard jawline?

Patience had dressed in casual slacks and her favorite royal-blue sweater for a café supper. Somehow she'd expected Gil to wear a suit as usual. She'd never seen him dressed in jeans and a casual plaid shirt, open at the throat. Her gaze lingered on his neck. A small brown mole there captured her notice.

The young waitress in jeans and a white T-shirt approached them warily. "The special tonight is Salisbury steak and mashed potatoes and gravy. Salad and dessert included."

"I'll have that." Patience closed the menu. Too much was going on for her to be bothered being fussy about what she ordered.

"Me, too," Gil agreed, handing his menu to the waitress. He smiled at her and then pointedly at Patience.

Patience took the hint and forced herself to smile at Gil.

The waitress's gaze darted back and forth between them as if one of them concealed a live grenade. She poured two cups of decaf coffee and escaped them.

As they still stared at each other.

"So, Gil?" Patience prompted him, her voice low in her throat. His face looked smooth, without a hint of five o'clock shadow. Had he shaved again just for her? Did that mean something? "What can I do for you?"

"When did your mother arrive in town?" he asked, glancing around at the other tables and booths.

What? What's your game, Gil? She followed his sweeping attention over the small café, also glancing at the other patrons.

Caught staring at them, people looked away.

"You should know when my mother arrived." Patience couldn't conceal the umbrage that vibrated in her throat. "Haven't you been keeping tabs on me?"

"As a matter of fact, I haven't." Gil lifted his coffee cup. "I've been trying to figure out how to approach a new trial."

Patience bit her tongue, holding back her opinion of trying an innocent man twice. She traced her cup's smooth handle with her forefinger. "Have you tried to find out if any of the stolen items have appeared for sale?"

She glanced over at him. A lock of his bitter chocolate-colored hair had escaped and fallen onto his forehead. It beckoned her to push it back into place.

Gil returned her attention, his blue eyes narrowed. "I already told you I had sent out descriptions of the stolen items to state and national theft databases. It wasn't easy because Mrs. Perkins couldn't help at all.

I had to depend on Vincent Caruthers for information.''

"Vincent Caruthers?" In the act of lifting her cup, Patience paused. "The antique dealer that testified?"

"Yes." Gil nodded to an older woman walking past them toward the rear exit. "Only a month before the robbery, he had been asked to appraise Mrs. Perkins's antiques for market and insurance value."

"He's local, right?" Patience drew in her first hot sip of coffee, feeling Gil's intense concentration on her.

"Yes, his shop is only a few doors down from here."

Great. Patience rolled the rich brew over her tongue and grinned to herself.

The waitress delivered their salads and bread basket, still behaving as if she were serving an alleged spy team.

Does this woman expect me to bite? Patience mentally shook her head.

Vincent Caruthers, she'd visit him soon. She wondered if she should try to talk to the neighbor who'd wanted to buy some pieces from Mrs. Perkins. That would be more difficult. He didn't have a shop. She gave Gil an assessing look and then discarded the idea of telling him about Mr. Pulaski's involvement and suggestion about looking into local dealers. *Something tells me this man wouldn't appreciate it.*

"What did you want to ask me about your son?"

Patience glanced once more into Gil's eyes, entrapped by his thick dark lashes that contrasted so with his blue irises.

Gil took a deep breath and put down his fork. "Darby's mother and I married young, too young." His words rushed together as if he wanted to get them out and get this over with. "We were total opposites…"

This bit of revelation confused Patience. *Where is this going?*

He pursed his lips. "Anyway, we divorced when Darby was only two. You were right," he admitted in a grudging tone. "Darby has been the unwilling witness and sometimes participant in angry emotional scenes. His mother, my ex, knows just what buttons to push."

Patience let his words settle deep in her mind and heart. What an admission for this unbending man to make. She almost said something to this effect, but stopped herself. "I'm afraid," she temporized, "your situation isn't unique."

"That doesn't make it any easier on my son," Gil started again. "After the brief conversation you and I had about Darby at school…" He paused as though sorting out his thoughts. "Later that evening, I had to confront his mother about a safety issue. I was glad I had talked to you first. Your input helped me keep my son's well-being the focus, not my anger at my ex's carelessness."

Impressed by his apparent honesty, Patience listened as he told her the story of the motorcycle ride and the helmet. As he spoke, a foolish desire to touch his fingers, so near to hers on the table, blossomed. She refused to let her hand reach for his.

Instead, she focused on his intent. *Can I trust this man? Is he really just concerned about his son? Or does he have a hidden agenda of his own?*

"I'm grateful for your standing up to me and getting my attention." Gil didn't meet her eyes. "I don't want the divorce to affect Darby negatively. Or at least, more than it already has."

Patience had stopped eating. *This is the man who helped put me into the sticky situation I'm in.* And this man had done the impossible—he'd stirred her sympathy in spite of everything that had come between them.

"It's hard…" Gil's voice broke. "Seeing Darby want his mother and yet still to see the harm she does him when he is with her."

"Why did you get custody?" Patience propped her chin on her hand. She gazed at him, taking in all the subtleties—his neat haircut trying to tame natural waves, his straight nose and inviting mouth. Jerking her mind back to the conversation, she asked, "Was Darby's mother unfit?"

"Not in the legal definition." Gil pushed his back against the booth and rested his forearms on the edge of the table. "She didn't want custody of Darby—"

"She didn't?" Patience's eyes widened as she met his gaze.

"No, she said I better keep him. I could do more for him." He stared down at the tabletop.

Patience considered this as she looked at his bowed head. She'd known what it felt like to be rejected by both her mother and the man who'd fathered her. Did Darby sense that his mother had relinquished him without a fight? Or was it hurtful only because his mother lived apart from him? "That explains a lot about your son."

"How do you mean?"

"His love cup is nearly empty. He longs for love and especially to be noticed. That's why he is acting out. He feels a compulsion, a craving for special attention to make up for the emptiness. And, unfortunately, this usually comes out as misbehavior." Patience lifted her fork.

"That much I already understand," Gil said in a self-deprecating tone. "But how do we stop his misbehavior?"

Patience folded her hands and stared at them, not Gil. Though he tempted her sorely. *Why do I want to be near him? Does it have anything to do with my concern for his son?* "I'm not a child psychologist, but I've learned a few things myself. First, how often do you hug Darby?"

"Hug him?" Gil looked as though she'd just asked something ridiculous.

She finally let herself touch his hand. *We all need to be touched, Gil.* ''You'd be surprised how healing the human touch can be. Even in these days where everyone is hypersensitive about misconduct, I try to touch my students hello and goodbye. A pat on the shoulder, on the head, the cheek. Just a touch can make a difference to a child.''

''I'll try to remember that.'' Gil's voice had roughened.

Was it with emotion?

She gazed into his eyes, seeing genuine vulnerability in this man. *He loves his son. He just wants what's best for him.*

She felt her heart move toward him. How could she be angry with a man who would bare his secrets and ask his enemy or at least, his least favorite person in town, for help with his son?

Gil folded his larger hand around hers.

''And you did right not making a big deal over the helmet in front of Darby.'' Her voice quivered with her reaction to his first tentative touch. ''But you still stood up to your ex-wife for your son's safety. I think you did pretty well in a difficult situation.''

''I did?'' He sounded pleased and his hand tightened around hers.

''You did.'' Her heart raced at their contact and she began to feel a lightness of spirit she hadn't felt in many days.

The waitress interrupted by serving their meals. Patience pulled her hand from Gil's. The young woman blushed…at catching them holding hands? She disappeared immediately.

Patience tried to focus on the meal in front of her, not thoughts of holding hands…and kisses. The aroma of beef floated up.

"I don't like my ex's new boyfriend." Gil picked up his knife and fork.

She tried to reel in her mounting curiosity about Gil. "Just because of the Harley?"

"No. The first time he met me he said that he and D.A.'s didn't get along."

I know how he feels. Patience allowed herself a wry grin. "Don't you think that might be just a reflex remark?"

"What do you mean?" He eyed her as if she spoke a foreign language.

"I'm sure your ex—what is her name?"

"Coreena."

"I'm sure Coreena had told him who you were in the community and he probably felt outclassed." Patience took a steadying sip of coffee and watched Gil's eyes, so revealing of his concern. "By throwing out that line, he was letting you know he won't be pushed around just because you have status he doesn't."

"You think so?"

"I do." Patience put her cup in the saucer and appraised him. Time to see if he would accept the advice he'd sought. "Now, how often does Darby visit his mother?"

"He spends every other weekend with her. She works at a supper club in the next town and makes sure she gets off two weekends a month."

A real sacrifice because her tips would be the best on the weekends. Do you realize that, Mr. District Attorney? "That means she does value her time with her son." Patience kept her voice even. "Do you ever prompt Darby to call his mom during the weeks they are apart?"

Gil's expression twisted. "No, I try to minimize their contact. It seems to upset him. He always acts up when he has to go to her place and when I pick him up."

"I think that's fairly common, too." Patience said a quick prayer. Giving advice was no small responsibility. "I think if you encourage Darby to have more consistent contact with his mom, the coming and going would be less of a…break or an emotional bump for him. And I think you'll find that he begins to feel better about himself."

"But she doesn't…"

"She doesn't what?" Patience studied his eyes, trying to read his struggle there. She imagined cupping his smooth cheek in her palm. She quickly refocused her thoughts on his son, where they belonged.

"She's…not a very good mother." The hesitant

words sounded wrung from him. He stared at his plate.

That's your opinion. Maybe she is and maybe she isn't, Gil. But I won't argue with you about that now. "But she *is* Darby's mother. You'll have to help her improve by encouraging what she does that is good and discouraging what is detrimental. Just like you did over her taking Darby out of school when he should have been serving detention."

"You heard about that?" Irritation flashed over his features.

I'm not prying into your affairs, Gil. "Of course...I'm his teacher. And after it happened, you put into place the procedure that Darby's mother isn't allowed to take him out of school without your permission."

"You sound like you think I overreacted."

Patience chewed, stalling. "I've never been a parent. But sometimes a special trip like that isn't a bad idea. I know that Darby was happier the next day. Maybe a day with his mom was just what he needed after the squirrel incident. Maybe his mom sensed that."

She observed from Gil's expression that this was a completely new idea to him.

The meal ended and Patience and Gil left the bright café for the dark night. At the corner of the square, Patience shivered in the bitter end-of-November wind.

"I can walk home alone. You're paying for a baby-sitter."

Gil didn't like the way she was dismissing him. Somewhere during the meal, this had become a date to him. Obviously not to Patience. "I could use the exercise and Darby likes his baby-sitter," he replied. "She'll play video games with him."

"Okay." Patience stepped off the curb and stumbled.

Gil caught her arm. "Careful."

"I'm okay. My heel hit a loose rock." She glanced around as they crossed the quiet street. "I hate it when it gets dark in winter so early."

Breathing in a fresh scent that clung to her skin, Gil kept her elbow in his grip.

At the other side, she tugged away from him.

Her pulling away disquieted him. Her blond hair shone in the darkness. And her pale face reflected the scant light from the street lamps. He drew nearer and kept in step with her. He tried to come up with some conversation, but his mind had gone blank. All he could think of was kissing Patience Andrews.

I can't kiss this woman. She's my son's teacher. And we're on the opposite sides of an ongoing case. But this line of reasoning didn't seem to dampen his urge to kiss this tall, willowy woman.

The street they walked along was deserted. Lights glowed in the windows of the houses they passed. A profound silence crowded in around them, broken only by an owl repeating its mournful call. Gil wrestled with his acute awareness of the woman beside him. *Why won't she look at me?*

"I appreciate your honesty," he said at last. They walked beside a high hedge in front of a large Victorian home.

"I appreciated yours."

Meee-ooow! A black cat sprang out in front of them from the hedge.

Patience leaped to one side, coming up against Gil.

His arms of their own accord wrapped around her. She turned within his arms, flush against his chest. And he kissed her.

He let his lips gently touch hers, drawing her warm breath into his own mouth. "Patience," he whispered. Shock rippled through him as she hesitated and then began to kiss him in return.

He drew her closer, closer, pressing her tightly against him. He wanted to trap her softness, her warmth there, keep it to warm him when he would again be alone.

"We shouldn't," she whispered.

He heard the halfhearted plea in her low voice, the voice that had attracted him from the first. "Right," he whispered back and he deepened his assault on her tender mouth.

A car drove by, momentarily bathing them in headlight glare. The intrusion broke their connection, but not their touch.

He was breathing hard. He shook himself mentally and gazed into Patience's face. She looked puzzled.

"I should be getting you home," he said, his voice rasping in his throat. But he refused to release her.

She nodded and they began walking again. This time, hand in hand. Only their gazes looked forward, not touching.

Finally on the front steps of Mrs. Honeycutt's, Patience said good-night to Gil. He still held her hand. She didn't know exactly what she should add…thanks for dinner and that kiss?

"Good night," he murmured and then he kissed her cheek. He swung away, hurrying down the steps and to the sidewalk without a backward glance.

But Patience couldn't move until he was swallowed up by the dark night. Then she let herself in quietly. She didn't want to bother her landlady. Or give in to the temptation to relate any of the confidential conversation she'd just had with Gil. Or reveal the fact that he'd kissed her.

She needed time to consider all he'd said to her. All she'd said to him. All he'd made her feel…

As she silently hung her coat on the hall tree, she heard voices coming from the open kitchen door at the other end of the front hall.

"I really appreciate the way you are standing behind my daughter," Patience's mother said.

"You have a fine girl," Bunny replied. From the sounds of water and clinking of china and silverware, she must have been washing dishes. "She's so busy, but she still volunteers at the Rose Care Center."

Patience didn't want to eavesdrop. She needed to make her presence known. But before she could speak up—

"My daughter is a good person," her mother said, "but none of that is my doing."

Patience froze. *No, no, don't…*

"Oh, Martina—"

"No, it's true," her mother interrupted Bunny. "You know I attend several AA meetings a week. I've got to stay dry this time. I've missed out on most of my only child's life. I don't want to miss the rest."

Jonesy sauntered out of the living room and approached Patience, purring. *Mother, please don't…*

"I find it hard to believe," Bunny insisted, "that you did as bad a job at mothering Patience as you seem to believe. She's a wonderful person."

Jonesy began rubbing Patience's pant legs. She stooped to pet the cat. What was it with cats and her tonight?

"I don't know how I could have done worse." Martina sighed loud and long. "I wasn't married to her father. I went from one destructive relationship to another throughout her childhood. And then when Patience was fifteen, I married Chet, a fellow drunk, and she ran away."

Patience stroked Jonesy, fighting her angry reaction to this revealing recital. Resentment of the past gripped her taut nerves in its gritty palm. *How can it still hurt me, Lord?*

"Oh, dear." Bunny's voice was filled with distress.

"If it hadn't been for my brother, Mike," Patience's mother continued, "I don't know what would have happened to Patience. He went and found her and took her to live with him."

"I think Patience has mentioned her uncle Mike."

"She loves him." Her mother paused.

Yes, I do. He's the one adult who really loved me, the only one in my family. You never have loved me, Mother. You don't know how. Even as Patience thought these accusations, she felt guilt over holding on to her grudge, her anger. Jonesy stretched, begging to be picked up. *How do I get rid of these bad feelings, Lord? They make me sick.*

And then her mother went on, "Sometimes I wonder how Mike and I could come from the same family. He's a hardworker, a God-fearing man in the best sense of the word."

Patience had wondered this, too. But Uncle Mike said it was all the work of God, his Holy Spirit.

"And I've been AWOL for most of Patience's life," her mother finished with something like a gasp.

Patience picked up Jonesy and cuddled his soft fur close against her cheek. Was Martina crying, trying to get Bunny's sympathy so that when she fell off the wagon, Bunny would already feel sorry for her? Patience couldn't trust her mother.

"Well, you're here now," Bunny said in a bracing tone. "That's what matters."

Mother, how could you dump everything like that? Still trapped in the foyer, Patience felt vulnerably exposed. Her mother had revealed facts about Patience that she didn't want anyone to know. Embarrassment shimmered through her in hot insistent waves. She hid her face in Jonesy's golden fur.

Dear Lord, I know the truth shouldn't bother me, but I don't like looking back. Uncle Mike taught me that much. And I know I should show love toward my mother, but how can I? Can't I just leave all this in the past where it belongs?

Back home after leaving Patience at Mrs. Honeycutt's, Gil paid the baby-sitter and looked at Darby, who was playing a video game on the floor in front of the TV. Gil recalled Patience's advice to him. More hugging. More contact with his mother.

More contact… Tonight's kiss replayed in his mind. Why had he let go of Patience? Why hadn't he asked her to…to what? *Where is this going?*

Patience disagreed with him, but that didn't keep her from trying to help him. Not a small, petty person, Miss Andrews. She acted as if she didn't like him. But why would she have let him kiss her and even responded to him if that were the case?

Well, let's see if her advice works. "Hey, Darby, want to call your mom?" Then he remembered Coreena would probably be working tonight. "If she's not home, you can leave her a good-night message."

His son looked up at him. Puzzlement was plain on the boy's face. "Can I?"

"Sure. Come on." Gil motioned his son toward the phone in the kitchen.

"I can dial it," Darby insisted, fixing his dad with a stare.

"Okay. Go ahead."

"Are you going to listen?" Frowning, Darby climbed onto the kitchen chair to reach the wall phone.

"Do you want me to?"

"No, I want to talk private." Darby waited with the receiver in his hands.

"Okay, I'll wait for you in your bedroom. It's time we got you in bed." Gil walked out of the room and down the hall. And then, feeling some guilt but unable to resist, he waited inside the open door to hear what his son would say.

Darby punched the buttons. Pause. "Hello, Mommy, this is Darby. Daddy said I could call you and say good night. I wish you were here so you could sing me to sleep like you do when I stay at your house. Okay. Say hey to Blaine for me. 'Night."

She sings him to sleep? Gil moved quickly to sit on the bed so his son wouldn't find him hovering near the door. Then Gil recalled Coreena singing to Darby as an infant when she'd cradled him in her arms. The memory brought shivers to him; Coreena's singing voice had always been low and sweet. *I didn't know she still did that, Darby.*

Then Patience's low, innocently enticing voice played in his mind also. He'd never realized that he was so sensitive to the sound of a woman's voice. Interesting.

He turned his mind back to the present. The baby-sitter had already gotten Darby into his pajamas. But Gil oversaw the last bathroom trip and the brushing of teeth. Then he sat at the end of his son's bed and watched Darby slide his feet under his comforter.

"Would you like me to read you a story?"

Darby eyed him. "Okay."

"Do you have a request?" Gil asked.

"The Little Engine That Could."

"Good choice." Gil reached for the book on the shelf at the end of the bed. He slid up to sit beside Darby, his back resting against the padded headboard.

Patience came to mind again and he put his arm around his son so that Darby leaned against him as he read his son's favorite story. Gil couldn't read Darby's mind, but this closeness felt like a benediction on the day. An armful of warm little son eased through Gil, helping him relax.

When he finished, he pressed a kiss onto the top of his son's dark head and then stroked the fine hair. "Now it's time for lights out. Sunday school in the morning. Good night. Sleep tight."

"Good night, Dad." Darby gave him a boisterous hug.

Gil hugged him tightly in return. Then he got up and turned off the light and walked out, thinking again of Patience's words.

Gil had liked the happy expression Darby had worn when he'd run to the phone to call his mom and leave her a message. *Why didn't I think of that before?*

She's right so far. Darby does need more hugging. He remembered again the sensation of holding the slender, lovely teacher in his arms only an hour ago. He needed more hugging, too. What would Miss Andrews say to that?

The telephone ringing woke Gil from a sound sleep. He groped for the bedside phone and picked up. He squinted at the clock—1:36 a.m. "Gil Montgomery."

"Hi, Gil, this is Sheriff Longworthy. Got bad news for you."

Gil sat up in bed. "What is it?"

"Another robbery. And it's just like the Putnam one."

"What? You're kidding." Gil shoved back his tousled hair.

"I'm not joking." Frustration leaked from the sheriff's voice. "We got a call an hour ago. A neighbor woke up and saw that a Mrs. Carmichael's lights were all on well after midnight. The neighbor knew that Mrs. Carmichael never leaves a light on that isn't being used and that she's usually in bed by eight every night.''

"Okay. So?" Gil massaged his forehead where a headache was starting.

"The neighbor couldn't get back to sleep, so he finally got dressed and went over. He found the back door open and Mrs. Carmichael on the floor unconscious, bound and gagged.''

Gil sucked in air. "*No*. How badly was she hurt?''

"I don't know. She was breathing but still unconscious when the ambulance took her to the hospital.''

"Let's hope she doesn't have a stroke like Mrs. Perkins.'' *Please God, no,* Gil prayed. "What was stolen?''

"Unclear as yet," Longworthy said, sounding angrier with each word, "but the house had been ransacked. I'm phoning from outside the kitchen on my cell phone. After sending deputies over the neighborhood looking for any suspicious persons, I've roped off the crime scene. I'm going to go over every inch of this kitchen and downstairs myself.''

"Good.'' Gil reached for a pen. "What's the address?''

"It's 246 Walnut.''

"That just can't be. It's down the street from Mrs. Perkins's.''

"You got it," the sheriff growled. "I'm going to go over this scene with a fine-tooth comb. Somebody's decided to copy Dan Putnam.''

Or somebody has attacked two women now. Was Patience right? That couldn't be. It couldn't be. But Dan Putnam is still in jail.

"I'm going to catch the dirty low-down skunk, copycat." Longworthy's voice vibrated with suppressed outrage. "We don't need any more complications in the first case."

"Right." *You said it.* "Make sure you have at least two witnesses with you as you gather evidence. I don't want anything compromised."

"No kidding. And when I'm done, I'm leaving a deputy here so no one tampers with the crime scene after I've collected all I can on the first sweep-through. I'll come back later and do it all again."

"I'd come over myself," Gil explained, "but I can't leave Darby. I'll come first thing in the morning."

"Okay, I'll tell the deputy to expect you."

The next morning after Gil dropped Darby at Sunday school and told him to go home with his grandfather, he drove to 246 Walnut to see if the sheriff had been right. Had someone copied Putnam? If so, why? He met the deputy at the back door.

"The sheriff said you'd be coming over." The young man who stood inside opened the door and let Gil in.

Gil didn't blame him for keeping watch from inside. It was a raw gray November morning. It reflected

Gil's mood. "Did the sheriff finish with the crime scene?" Gil almost didn't want to enter the house. *This can't be happening.*

"Not completely." The deputy looked frustrated, too. "He said he needed a break. He only left about a half hour ago. Said he'd have breakfast and then be back for another sweep. He doesn't want to miss anything."

"Good." Gil pulled himself together. "I'll just take a quick look inside then. I don't want to disturb anything." He walked farther into the kitchen. The room showed that an investigation had begun. All the surfaces showed fingerprinting dust.

Drawers that must have been pulled out by the robber and left showed evidence of a hasty search. A kitchen chair lay on its side in the center of the room. On the nearby table, a coil of cording had been tagged and bagged. The label on its clear plastic bag read: Cord found around victim's wrists and ankles. Another contained a soiled dishcloth. Its tag read: Gag From Victim's Mouth.

Gil stepped into the doorway to the next room and was met by a scene of destruction—furniture overturned, objects lying shattered, sofa cushions ripped apart.

The sheriff hadn't been mistaken. The scene looked just like Mrs. Perkins's home had after the robbery. *What does this mean?*

Gil turned to go. He couldn't do much here. This

part of the investigation belonged to the sheriff. At the back door, he stopped to speak to the deputy. ''If the sheriff comes back before I do, tell him I've gone to the hospital to see how Mrs. Carmichael is doing.''

The deputy nodded.

Gil shuffled down the back-porch steps and scanned the quiet, old neighborhood. *What's going on, Lord? Why did someone copy Dan Putnam? And please, please let Mrs. Carmichael be able to answer questions.*

Chapter Seven

Gil waited at the corner of the town square, watching parishioners, bundled up in somber winter coats and scarves, walking down the steps of the red brick church. Icy wind made his ears ache. Stomping his chilled feet, he looked away whenever anyone glanced toward him. This had been his church before his divorce. He hadn't felt welcome since then because some members had made sure he didn't.

He wouldn't have come here, but the compulsion to tell Patience about the second robbery had overwhelmed his better instincts. He wanted to be here. He wanted to be a thousand miles away. He didn't move.

Finally, through the thinning crowd, he glimpsed the short blond hair he'd been seeking. He pushed away from the oak he'd been leaning against and moved to the bottom of the steps.

Patience paused one step above him and looked down into his eyes.

Her expression made his mouth dry. *Does she have any idea how she affects me?*

She lifted one eyebrow.

Then he said what he'd come to say. "There's been a second robbery."

She was at his side. "Tell me."

Her nearness wrapped itself around him, an alien warmth, a brightness he couldn't resist. That's what had really brought him here, to her. "A neighbor of Mrs. Perkins was attacked in her home last night."

"Is she all right?"

Her quick sympathy drew him closer. "I stopped at the hospital before coming here. She's still unconscious but she should be all right. The doctor didn't think she'd sustained any lasting hurt."

"Thank God."

He nodded. Her long graceful neck was bent toward him. His fingers tingled, wanting to ruffle through the golden wisps of hair on her nape.

"So did Dan Putnam break out of county jail last night to commit this crime?" Her tone was arch.

He'd expected her to take this line. He paused and she followed suit. He stood just inches from her, his gaze taking in the pale pink of her lips and the light blush of excitement on her face. "The sheriff believes this is the work of a copycat."

"Why would someone copy a crime?" She fixed

him with an intense expression. Her lips pouted and he remembered their softness on his own.

His whole body tensed. *She never takes things lightly. Why does she care so much? She's almost a stranger here.* He shrugged off her question, refusing to let her see how she intrigued him. "Maybe because it worked."

"It didn't work very well, did it, since Dan Putnam was arrested almost immediately? Why would someone want to copy his disastrous example?"

He even liked the way she challenged him at every turn. No breathy feminine coaxing, no playful glances, no flirting at all. Patience just came right back at him.

"We were able to catch Putnam," he said, "because he had a connection to his mother. Relatives are usually the first suspects in an assault case."

"I'll keep that in mind." Her rich voice dipped into scathing disapproval. She started walking briskly away from him. "I hope nothing happens to *my* mother."

It took him a moment to process her comment. A few long strides and he caught up with her. What had caused that? It wasn't like her. "That was a low blow." He gripped her elbow.

She hesitated, her face lowered. "You're right. I apologize."

"Then I'll admit—" he forced himself to say the words "—that this does call Putnam's guilt into question."

She made eye contact with him. "Thank you."

With slight pressure on her arm, he urged her to start walking again. "I still think the sheriff is right. This is a copycat crime." *I can't have been so wrong about Putnam. I know he's guilty and I'll prove it in the next trial.* "I just wanted you to hear this from me."

"I appreciate that." She walked beside him, staring forward. A frown marked her profile. "But I don't agree with you. Will you promise me something?"

"What?" He almost shied away from making the obvious reply. *I don't want to promise you anything, Patience.* But he knew he lied. He longed to make promise after promise to her....

"That you won't look at the evidence and try to make it fit into a copycat crime." She held him captive in her glance. "Will you try to look at this robbery as a separate incident?"

His cell phone rang, saving him from responding. He pulled it from his pocket. When he'd finished his conversation, he turned to her. He didn't like not answering her question. But he didn't want to discuss this any longer. But more than that, motivated him, his desire to keep her with him.

He wanted to kiss her, here on the square and with Sunday-church traffic all around them. That would send the tongues wagging.

"Mrs. Carmichael has regained consciousness. The

sheriff is going to question her. Would you like to come along with me and observe?''

''Me?''

''Yes.'' *You are an unusually perceptive person. And you're right. I need to look at this with new eyes. Maybe your presence will keep me from missing an important bit of evidence. And I'll have you with me for a few more minutes.*

She studied him as though she easily read his thoughts. ''Very well.''

In a few steps, he led her to his car parked on the square. He drove them the few miles to the local hospital and then checked his watch. At home with his granddad, Darby would need lunch soon.

Gil met the sheriff, bleary-eyed from lack of sleep, in the corridor outside Mrs. Carmichael's room. The sheriff looked surprised to see Patience, who stood a bit behind Gil.

Patience greeted the sheriff in a subdued voice.

The sheriff nodded to her. ''The doc says we can only stay for about three minutes. She's really shook up and is on pain meds.''

''I understand.'' Gil followed the sheriff into the room, shepherding Patience inside with a hand at the small of her back. He dropped his arm and proceeded forward.

The pale older woman in the bed watched them approach. A nurse was checking her pulse.

"I just have a few questions, Mrs. Carmichael," the sheriff said from the other side of the bed.

"I don't feel much like talking," the older woman whimpered.

Patience stood close to Gil, her fragrance—flowers and cinnamon—contrasted with the antiseptic hospital smells.

"Did you see your assailant?" the sheriff began.

"No, I walked into the kitchen and something hit me in the head from behind. It hurt." Her voice quavered. "That's all I remember."

"About what time would that have been?" Gil made himself ask.

The woman turned her pale blue eyes to him, a tear spilling down her lined cheek. "I was going to take my bedtime pills and then turn in, so it must have been right after Lawrence Welk on PBS."

"About 7:30 p.m.?" the sheriff asked for clarification.

"Yes." Mrs. Carmichael began weeping. Her hands shook as she wiped away tears.

"Was your back door locked at that time?" the sheriff went on.

"No, I always lock it after I take my pills." She began crying harder.

Brushing past Gil, Patience reached for the woman's wrinkled hand and gripped it. "I'm so sorry this happened to you."

"We won't bother you anymore now," Gil apologized. "Rest."

The woman ignored him. She blinked away the tears and stared up into Patience's face. "You're that teacher who stopped Dan Putnam from being found guilty."

"Yes, I am."

"Well, I thought you were crazy." The woman sniffled, still trying to stop crying. "But now I think you were right. If Dan Putnam's in county jail, he can't have attacked me."

"Mrs. Carmichael," Gil objected, "it's too soon to tell if this has anything to do with the Putnam case."

"Why?" Mrs. Carmichael asked.

Patience continued to hold her hand, but turned to observe him.

Gil took a step closer to Patience. It was time to draw her away. "We'll keep you posted on developments," he added, trying to project a confidence he didn't feel.

On the next Thursday afternoon after school, the little bell over the door jingled as Patience let herself into the Shop on the Square. On the door in gilt lettering appeared the name Vincent Caruthers, Dealer of Fine Antiques.

The shop had an austere look to it. No embroidered linens, ladies' gloves or frilly hankies displayed within the glass counters. Instead, there were a few

Love Inspired®

"When I found these Love Inspired novels, I found hope."

– Beverly D., Buffalo, NY

LETTERS FROM READERS
WHOSE HEARTS WERE
TOUCHED BY OUR
UNIQUE BRAND OF
INSPIRATIONAL ROMANCE.

Now it's your turn to fall in love with

> "We all need a little romance in our lives and this wholesome, inspirational series is exactly what I have been looking for."
> – Karen K., Warner, AB

> "It's a pleasure to read good, interesting, clean in thought, word and character books."
> – Bonnie L., Basile, LA

> "I love this series. It lifts my spirits."
> – Laura R., Nanuet, NY

> "Thank you...I will not be ashamed to share these with my granddaughter who has become interested in reading since she always sees me with a book close by."
> – M.L., Joshua Tree, CA

Scratch the silver area, complete and return the card on the right to receive your 2 FREE *Love Inspired®* books.

These books have a combined cover price of $9.00 in the U.S. and $10.50 in Canada, but they are yours free!

SPECIAL FREE GIFT!
No obligation!
No purchase necessary!

We'll send you a fabulous surprise gift, absolutely FREE, simply for accepting our no-risk offer!

Visit us online at
www.LoveInspiredBooks.com

Each of your *FREE* Love Inspired titles is filled
with joy, faith and family values.

Scratch off the silver area
to see what the Steeple
Hill Reader Service has
waiting for you!

YES! Please send me the **2 FREE** Love Inspired® books
and **FREE GIFT** for which I qualify. I understand that I am under
no obligation to purchase any books as explained on the back
of this card.

313 IDL DVG2   113 IDL DVGZ

FIRST NAME	LAST NAME

ADDRESS

APT.#	CITY

STATE/PROV.	ZIP/POSTAL CODE

(LI-TE-04)

Steeple Hill Reader Service™—Here's How It Works:

If offer card is missing write to: Steeple Hill Reader Service, 3010 Walden Ave., P.O. Box 1867, Buffalo NY 14240-1867

BUSINESS REPLY MAIL
FIRST-CLASS MAIL   PERMIT NO. 717-003   BUFFALO, NY

POSTAGE WILL BE PAID BY ADDRESSEE

STEEPLE HILL READER SERVICE
3010 WALDEN AVE
PO BOX 1867
BUFFALO NY 14240-9952

NO POSTAGE
NECESSARY
IF MAILED
IN THE
UNITED STATES

good pieces of art deco jewelry, watch fobs and cuff links. A man's shop. But every piece of wood glowed and the scent of lemon oil hung in the air. Patience walked past a display of very good, very expensive American primitive pieces: a homemade pie safe, a Windsor rocker with an aged patina, a carved highboy painted turkey red.

"May I be of help?" A tall fiftyish man with a serious face stepped from the rear of the store.

"I'm just looking." Patience used the standard reply of all browsers. *For clues about you and what you might have done.*

"Well, that's a good start." He gave her a prim grin. "Take your time. If anything interests you, please alert me. If you are looking for a certain type of collectible or antique, also let me know. I go to many sales and auctions."

"Thanks. I will." Then Patience took her time looking over everything the shop had to offer. All the while, she pondered Vincent Caruthers. She'd come primarily to get an impression of him as a possible suspect. And something about her impression of him today dissatisfied her. Or was it just her already aroused suspicion?

In the midst of her inspection of an interesting mahogany secretary, the phone call she'd gotten this morning came back to her. Out of the blue, Sprague, Putnam's lawyer, had contacted her. "You've heard about the second robbery, haven't you?" he'd asked.

She'd assented and then he'd dropped his bomb-shell. "I've been watching you, wondering if you could be of help to me with my defense in the second trial." That was all he'd said, but had he implied more?

Did Sprague want her to pick Gil's brain and then feed information to him? The thought hit Patience badly. She'd agreed to nothing and ended the con-versation quickly.

But I am trying to find facts to help Dan Putnam. Would it be wrong to give the defense lawyer anything Gil tells me? That didn't sound right to her. *But who would I tell if I actually find something? It would have to be Sprague or it won't do Dan Putnam any good.*

Finally, with a knitted forehead, she walked to the back of the store and was met by the proprietor. "Do you ever evaluate items for insurance or sale value?"

"I do sometimes." Caruthers led her toward the center of the shop beside a display of an Early Amer-ican maple dining-room set, replete with a full rose-chintz china set.

"I have some pieces of jewelry from a great-grandmother put away in a safe-deposit box in Chi-cago," Patience said her practiced speech. She'd had to come up with a reason for meeting again with Mr. Caruthers. Browsing over and over and not buying would look suspicious.

"So you're the new teacher from the Windy City."

Caruthers gazed at her with a glint of what...in his eyes?

"Yes." She tried to smile disarmingly. "And I'm sure you're aware that I'm the one who was responsible for the hung jury. You must have seen me in the jury box."

"Of course. I wouldn't have missed such a pretty face, especially in such dismal surroundings."

She looked as if his compliment pleased her. It didn't. "I'm sure it was unpleasant to be involved in a robbery case. Bad publicity for your shop."

He chuckled without humor. "They say any publicity is good publicity."

"And now Mrs. Carmichael has been robbed." She made her voice very innocent. "I hope you didn't do any evaluations for her."

The man eyed her and started walking her toward the store's front. "Is that supposed to be an accusation?"

"No." But she let him lead her to the door. "How could you have anything to do with robbery? Before I came in, I asked around about your reputation. You have an excellent one. But unfortunately, there are some disreputable antique dealers. I always like to know with whom I'm doing business."

"Ah. And are we going to be doing business?" He reached for the doorknob.

"Maybe," Patience hedged, wondering if he realized how guilty his body language looked as he ushered her so abruptly out of his presence. "I'm trying to decide whether or not to increase the insurance on my jewelry."

"I'd be happy to help in that. My appraisal fee is quite reasonable, I think." He quoted it and opened the door for her.

"Thank you." She paused to shake his soft hand. "I'll get back to you soon."

She stepped outside and bumped into Gil. Seeing him so unexpectedly shot through her like tiny darts. She wobbled slightly on impact.

"Patience." Gil steadied her by gripping her upper arms. "What are you doing here?"

She took a deep breath, knowing Mr. Caruthers was watching them. "I was consulting the dealer about his doing an appraisal for me."

Gil's eyes narrowed. "Oh?"

She slipped from his grasp. "Yes." She looked to the uniformed man beside Gil. "Hello, Sheriff."

He nodded.

"Yes, hello, sheriff," Caruthers said behind her, sounding less than thrilled to see the two men. "What can I do for you today?"

Sheriff Longworthy mumbled something and then entered the store, shutting the door behind him.

"Patience, can you come over to my place tonight?" Gil asked. "It's a school night, so I have to be there to put Darby to bed."

"Come to your house?" The suggestion jolted her.

"Why?" Sprague's conversation tightened her nerves. What did Gil want to tell her? Or glean from her?

Or was he going to kiss her again? Her face warmed at this last thought.

"I want to discuss this case with you." Gil didn't make eye contact with her.

He's not telling me something. What?

"The sheriff just gave me his full report on Mrs. Carmichael's crime scene," Gil continued, talking to a point above her left ear. "Today she's back home from staying at her daughter's."

"Do you think it's wise for me to come to your house?" Patience asked. Was this another ploy in his attempt to show that they got along in spite of the gossip over her being responsible for the hung jury? Now though, she had another worry. *Gil, I know you're a danger to me, to my feelings. And what are you keeping from me?*

"Darby will be pleased if his teacher visits."

She had to grin at this. "Very well. How about seven?"

"Fine. I'll drive over and pick you up—"

"I can walk."

"I'll pick you up."

She shook her head. "Everything always has to be your way, doesn't it?" She walked away from him. But she couldn't walk away from the effect he'd had on her.

* * *

"When'er we getting our tree?" Darby asked Gil as he pulled in front of Mrs. Honeycutt's house later that day just before 7:00 p.m.

"I'll discuss that with you later." Gil's body hummed with anticipation. He would have Patience beside him within moments. But for how long after he told her what the sheriff had discovered? "Now I have to go get Miss Andrews."

"Why's my teacher coming to our house?" Darby grumbled again.

"I told you why." Gil didn't like repeating his reason—to discuss the new case—because he felt guilty that he might be lying to the boy and himself. Certainly the unexpected evidence would garner a distinct reaction from Miss Patience Andrews. Gil shut the car door against the chill night and his mind against all the what-ifs his brain had churned out. He hurried up the walk and steps to the front door.

Patience met him there. She looked strained. She looked lovely.

This thought rattled him. *I'm courting disaster here. Do I really want to consult with this woman? Or is this just an excuse to be near her? What will she say when I tell her?*

Without a word, she walked down the steps beside him. Brain dead, he couldn't think of a thing to say to her. He opened the car door and she slid past him onto the front seat, her subtle scent tempting him.

"Hi, Miss Andrews," Darby called out from his place in the back seat.

"Good evening, Darby."

Gil got in beside her and started the car. He made himself concentrate on the dark street ahead, though his awareness of the young woman beside him threatened his focus on driving.

I can't let myself be interested in this woman. I have a son to raise. And an ex-wife in town with a boyfriend who has a criminal record. That's enough to deal with.

"Teacher," Darby piped up from the back seat, "are you going to get a Christmas tree?"

"Mrs. Honeycutt, my landlady, is going to get one. I'll enjoy hers."

"I want a real one," Darby replied. "I want to cut it down with my dad and grandpa."

"That sounds like fun." Patience glanced over her shoulder at Darby.

Not looking toward me. So this attraction is just happening to me? He tightened his grip on the wheel. *So I can kiss her and it's no big deal to her.* The fact grated inside him like twisting a stubborn rusty bolt.

"But we gotta wait. It's too soon." Darby sounded bereft.

"Maybe it's too soon for the tree, but how about lights?" Patience turned from his son and cast Gil an appraising look.

"Lights?" Gil met her eyes.

"Yes." Patience looked as though she was trying to tell him something beyond her words. "Don't you put up any lights in your windows?"

"Lights?" Gil repeated.

"Yes, if your father doesn't object, let's stop here and pick up a string of lights." Patience pointed to the drugstore just ahead on the square. "My treat."

"Whoopee!" Darby hooted. "Christmas lights."

"But—" Gil began.

"Sorry, I should have asked you first." Patience touched his arm. Her contact drove all thought—and resistance—from his mind. He pulled into the parking place in front of the drugstore. Darby clambered out of the back seat.

With Gil at their heels, Patience and his son walked into the drugstore and picked out a string of multi-colored lights and four suction-cup hooks.

Gil insisted on paying for them and then followed Patience and Darby outside, aware that everyone in the drugstore had been gawking at them. *Why did we do that? Why are we buying Christmas lights the second week in December? We never have Christmas lights.*

"We never had Christmas lights before." Darby echoed his dad's unspoken words.

"Well, it's nice to have a bit of holiday cheer early in December," Patience said. "I love everything about Christmas."

"Me, too!" Darby gave one of his little jumps.

"What about you, Gil?" Patience gazed at him.

He swallowed a lump that had gathered near his Adam's apple. "Who doesn't like Christmas?" But he did dread Christmas—and all the deal-making with Coreena and maneuvering of Darby between two houses. But this woman didn't need to know anything of that.

Gil drove home, and walking into the kitchen he was met by his dad. The three of them shed their winter jackets. "Oh, hi. I didn't know we'd be seeing you tonight."

"I told Darby I'd help him with his subtraction tonight." His dad stared hard at Patience.

"Good evening, Captain Montgomery." Patience offered him her hand. "Darby and I are going to put some Christmas lights up in his room."

The Captain shook her hand, but looked glum.

"His room?" Gil couldn't keep surprise out of his voice.

"Of course." Patience wondered why Gil had to question or counter everything she suggested. *We're not in court, Gil.* "Then when Darby goes to bed, he can enjoy them while he falls to sleep. Where's your room, Darby?"

Darby grabbed her hand and dragged her down the hall to his bedroom. Two walls of his room were painted white and two navy blue. Sports posters dotted the walls. And toys, mostly Lego, littered the navy blue carpet.

Gil stood in the doorway, an observer, not a participant.

Gil, come on. Patience wanted to shake him.

"What a nice room." Patience saw that Gil's dad had followed them and was standing in the doorway glaring at her. "Darby, which window do you want them in?"

"These toys should have been picked up before your teacher came," the Captain barked.

Patience sent a glance toward Gil again and he walked over to her.

Paying no attention to anyone but Patience, Darby pointed to the window over his headboard.

"But then you won't be able to see them when you are in bed," Patience said.

"Okay. That window." Darby pointed to the window on the other wall across from his bed.

"Good choice." Feeling Gil's intense concentration on her, Patience began to blush and was glad she had her profile to him.

Within minutes, she and Gil's son had worked the string of lights out of the box, licked and stuck the suction-cup hooks onto the four corners of the window, and strung the lights and plugged them in.

"Wow," Darby crowed. "Wait till I tell Mommy that I've got Christmas lights in my bedroom."

Gil patted his son on the head. "They do add something to the room."

Finally. Patience moved toward the door.

"Okay, let's get to that subtraction," Gil's dad growled at Darby.

Darby nodded. He and his grandfather sat down at the desk on one side of the room.

Patience noted though that Darby's eyes kept flicking back to the colored lights glinting against the window. How did Darby get along with his grandfather, a gruff man to be sure.

"Okay, let's get down to business, Patience," Gil said and let her precede him down the hallway.

She tried to let the feeling of the house speak to her about the man and his son who lived here. She got the impression of busyness and lack of time. In the kitchen, Patience reached out and touched Gil's arm. "Before we start, there's something I need to tell you."

Chapter Eight

G il stared at Patience, trying to read her expression for any hint of what she was talking about. Tonight— already filled with all kinds of possible repercussions—now cranked up another notch of tension. "What is it?"

"Dan Putnam's lawyer called me recently." She slid her small hand from his arm and lowered her eyes.

Missing her touch, Gil motioned for her to sit at the table. After she sank onto the maple chair, he eased down around the corner of the table near her. Her subtle scent beckoned him. "What did Sprague want?"

"He wants me to pass on to him anything I hear or dig up that might help his client." Patience wouldn't meet his eyes. Her thick golden-brown lashes fanned over her cheeks.

He gazed at the lovely picture she made, sitting so close. "Well..." *Why did that surprise you?* "Weren't you already planning on doing that?"

"I hadn't thought about it." Her sober eyes lifted to his. "But of course, I would...probably."

"So..." Gil spread his hands on the table, palms up.

"It doesn't seem right somehow." Patience's face twisted with concentration. "I want Dan Putnam to have a second chance. I think he will be vindicated."

"You've mentioned that before." Gil made his voice dry and casual. He noted one of her hands rested on the table just inches from his.

"Maybe it feels like tale-bearing," Patience said at last. "Like I talk with you and you take me into your confidence and then I go and repeat what you've told me to a third party. It feels...wrong."

"But how were you going to help Dan?" Gil posed the obvious question. He moved his restless hand a centimeter nearer hers.

"I guess I thought I wouldn't be getting any help from you." She gazed at him across the mere inches that separated them.

"Ah." Gil let himself grin. "If it helps any, I really don't plan on giving you information about Dan Putnam." The something he needed to know popped back into his mind. *Go ahead and ask her while she's still speaking to you.* "Why were you at Vincent Caruthers's shop today?"

"I told you why. Don't you believe me?" She withdrew from him, pressing her spine against the chair back, laying her hands in her lap—out of his reach. She repeated, "I was thinking of having him do an appraisal for me."

"Is that all?" Folding his arms, he didn't try to keep the skepticism from his tone.

She lifted her chin. "Is that why I'm here? So you can scold me about meddling again?"

"No." No need to get her back up already. "I wanted to go over with you the evidence the sheriff managed to glean from the second robbery."

"Why?" Patience asked, looking suspicious.

"Because I expect to persuade you that there really isn't a connection between the two crimes." *And I want you to hear the worst from me. No one else.* Should he tell her right away or keep the really disturbing facts till last?

He answered his own question and drew back one last time from the unpleasant task, reluctant to cause her pain and embarrassment.

Patience looked to him still.

"Okay, then." He tried to keep his focus on the task he'd set for himself and not the enticing woman at the table. He lifted a folder off the nearby counter and laid it open on the table. "Let's go over the crime scene report."

"What did the sheriff find out?" Patience glanced at the typed pages in front of them.

"First, the perpetrator must have a personal knowledge of Mrs. Carmichael's routine. The neighbor who called in to alert the police about her lights being on only demonstrated that Mrs. Carmichael had a very predictable schedule," he said as he admired Patience's simple hairstyle, so natural and not in the least flamboyant like his ex-wife's. "The robber must have known that Mrs. Carmichael would enter the kitchen after her favorite Saturday-night show and he was waiting in just the right spot in the kitchen to knock her out without being seen."

"I see," Patience said with a fixed stare, as though her mind grappled with the information. "That makes sense. Did Mrs. Carmichael have any idea who might have known her routine?"

"Many people." He bent and flicked the pointed edge of the pages with his thumb, making a thrumming-ticking sound. "Her reputation for never varying from her habits was, I suppose you could say, a standing joke among her family and neighbors." No one was laughing now, though.

"So that means even someone who wasn't close to the lady could have known about her sticking to her weekly schedule?" Patience glanced to him.

Her brown eyes appeared richer in the low light of the kitchen. Beautiful eyes. He shook himself mentally. "Right. The sheriff finally compiled the list of stolen items. It consists of antique jewelry—a diamond-and-ruby brooch and a gold-and-diamond pendant that had belonged to Mrs. Carmichael's great-grandmother, and around eight hundred dollars in cash—''

"That much," Patience gasped.

Gil nodded. "People who lived through the Depression still like to keep cash on hand, I guess." He glanced at the notes again. "And a complete nineteenth-century sterling-silver tea set."

"Whoa," she breathed. "Those can be expensive."

He shut his mouth tight. Patience's presence was working on him more and more. *I don't want to continue this conversation. Do I have to tell her?*

"So the same type of items that were stolen from Mrs. Perkins were also taken from Mrs. Carmichael?" she asked.

"We've already told you we think someone has copied the original crime," he reminded her gently. *I have to go ahead regardless.*

"Did you find any hard evidence connecting anyone to this crime?" She leaned forward.

He had expected her to ask this, a dangerous question, though she didn't realize it. Still, this query was his cue.

Silently apologizing, he looked into her shining, innocent eyes and forced himself to go on. "The sheriff fingerprinted every possible surface in the house, especially in the areas where evidence of a pilfering were obvious. Mrs. Carmichael and her neighbors and relatives gave us samples of their prints so we could eliminate those.''

"Why did you automatically cross Mrs. Carmichael's relatives off the list of suspects?" Her tone became tarter. "You didn't *eliminate* Dan Putnam as a suspect just because he was a relative. In fact, you told me you suspected him because of his relationship to his mother and, of course, his fingerprints would be in her house.''

She doesn't miss a trick. Again, her no-nonsense, don't-lie-to-me ways pleased him. "In this case, we couldn't find any animosity between anyone amongst the local family members.''

"Just because you didn't find it right away doesn't mean it might not exist," Patience muttered. "People don't always wash their family's dirty laundry where everyone can see.''

Her nearly prophetic comment gave him no relief. His insides had dipped heavier and heavier as though he had lead shot in his midsection. *This is going to be really unpleasant, and this evening she took the time to make my son happy again. I wish I could repay her for that. But to hear this from me is better than hearing it from the sheriff. Or some mean-spirited gossip.*

"The sheriff plans to dig into that possibility," he said gruffly, not willing to argue with her right now. "Maybe I shouldn't have used the word *eliminate*. I should have said, *identify*. We—the sheriff and I—are keeping an open mind on family involvement. We asked Cal Fiskus for a sample of his fingerprints and he refused us again. We checked Hank Drulow's— whose fingerprints are also on the national database— and they didn't match, either.''

''So did you find any fingerprints that didn't match friends and family?'' She sounded unconvinced.

The moment he'd been dreading. ''Yes, we did.'' He swallowed and stiffened himself to deliver the blow. ''We found two sets of fingerprints for which we had no immediate match.''

''Two?''

''Yes,'' he hurried on. ''One—a set of just a forefinger and a thumb—we still haven't been able to identify, but…'' He fell silent.

''But?''

''So, several of your mother's fingerprints were found at the crime scene—in an upstairs room where they shouldn't have been.'' He stared at the report and then forced himself to face her.

''My mother's fingerprints?'' Patience gaped at him. ''How did you find—''

''We entered them in the national database and she came up as a match.'' Pause. ''Why didn't you tell me your mother has a criminal record?''

Patience felt her throat dry up. Her tongue stuck to the roof of her mouth, she could only stare at him.

''Mrs. Carmichael has told us that your mother has been coming to her house weekly to demonstrate cosmetics to her. So your mother had been in the house with her permission—''

''And because she has a criminal record, she automatically becomes a suspect.'' Patience didn't even recognize the harsh voice as hers.

''Your mother is being investigated thoroughly as a person whose fingerprints were in the house and as a person who knew Mrs. Carmichael and her routine.'' Gil looked strained and uneasy. ''Don't you see? I wanted you to hear this from me and not the sheriff or read it in the newspaper.''

''The newspaper?'' Her parched throat nearly squeezed shut. ''It'll be reported in the newspaper?''

''It may be.'' He put his hand over hers where it clutched the table's edge. ''We won't give out our list of suspects, but there may be a leak. It can happen.''

''I might as well just resign and leave town right now.'' Patience ripped her hand from his. She shot up out of her chair.

''Wait.'' Gil stood up, too.

''People in town had started forgetting.'' She wanted to stop her voice from rising but it possessed its own mind and shrilled higher. ''They'd started looking at me as if I weren't public enemy number one. I can't face it all over again. Having people look at me like I'm dirt.''

He reached for her.

She stepped back, bumping against her chair. ''You read her whole record, didn't you?'' she accused him.

"Not just her most recent sentence for vehicular man-slaughter while driving drunk?"

Gil nodded, his eyes pitying her.

"Oh, no." Patience felt as if the words had been jerked out of her somewhere near her heart. She couldn't look at him. *I didn't want anyone to know. I left that all far behind me. Dear Lord, make this just a dream.* Her heart pounded in her ears. "I'm going now."

"No." Gil blocked her path. "No, don't leave like this. I wanted to shield you from this, but I couldn't."

She wrapped her arms around herself, edging back from him.

"I frankly couldn't believe it when I read it." His voice low, he leaned toward her. "You don't fit the profile of a person with an abusive childhood."

She glanced up at this, her face burning. She wanted to scream at him. Hit him. She wrestled with her rage. Moments filled with fury flamed through her. *I can't give in to emotion. I should have expected this. Wherever my mother goes she brings only pain and shame.*

She finally subdued her rage, sucking in deep even breaths. She couldn't let Gil know why this affected her so completely. He was merely the father of a student. Nothing more, and would never be anything more. His delving into her past had sealed that.

"Something obviously made a difference," he was saying. "I was shocked at your mother's charges—

child endangerment, neglect, abuse. Why didn't they take you away from her?''

She averted her eyes, but she couldn't hold back the acid words that frothed up from inside. ''Chicago's a big place, and in court my mom always did very well at remorse and enacting a convincing show of resolve to change her ways.'' She felt a sneer twist her features. ''But she never did.''

He said no word.

''I don't think she has now.'' Patience felt herself running out of steam. The shock had charged her anger, but it was impossible to sustain. ''She's been an alcoholic her whole adult life. She becomes violent when she's drunk. Every week she heads off to her AA meetings and I ask myself—how long will this dry spell last?'' Patience pressed a hand to her pounding forehead.

''You don't think that she's on the wagon for good?''

''You read her criminal record,'' Patience challenged him. ''What do you think?''

He made no reply and then said, ''She's your mother. You know her better than I do.''

''Yes, I do.'' *Unfortunately.*

Patience's crushed tone pushed Gil forward. He folded her into his arms, cradling her, wishing he knew more about comforting a woman. ''Let it go,'' he whispered.

She spent only one moment pushing at him, and then she drooped against his chest.

"Let it go. Whether your mother falls off the wagon or not is not your fault—"

Patience buried her face into the inviting fold between his jaw and shoulder and moaned, "Why did she have to come *here...now*?"

Gil held her, wishing he hadn't had to reveal this news, wishing he could have just expunged the record of the fingerprints as unpromising. *But I couldn't. Martina's got a long and unpleasant record and she's hard up for cash. She could have...*

He stopped his thoughts. He heard a small sob slip from Patience. *No, no, this has nothing to do with you. You're innocent of any wrongdoing. You show such love to my son. How are you able to do that? With a mother like yours, the textbooks say you shouldn't be such a kind, gentle, strong...*

He pressed small kisses along her hairline, feeling the silky softness of her feathery bangs and smooth skin under his lips. *You feel wonderful in my arms, Patience. I don't want to let you go.*

This last thought rocked him from the top of his head to the soles of his feet. *I can't let this start. We're in a sticky situation with these two cases. And now your mother's right in the middle of it.*

And I'm not the kind of man you deserve. I've got an ex-wife hanging around my neck and a child that needs all my attention. I'm a bad bet all around. You deserve better.

Still, he couldn't release her. His arms held her flush against him.

"You shouldn't be holding me," Patience murmured. Her voice had lost all its fire. And her actions belied her words. She remained within his embrace.

"I know I shouldn't," he whispered into her ear, just centimeters from his lips. He bent closer and kissed her mouth. As their lips pressed together, he found it hard to breathe. He savored her mouth, taking his time drawing out all the sweetness there.

The phone rang.

He tightened his hold on Patience, her soft form molded against him. But the mood had been shattered, and he released her. "Hello," he barked into the receiver.

"This is Coreena, Gil. Please, I need you. Will you come down to the courthouse?"

"What's wrong?"

"Blaine and I need you to put up our bail. We're in jail."

Gil stood at the entrance of the county jail. Patience waited at his elbow. Gil scanned the page of minor charges of disturbing the peace and disorderly conduct against his ex-wife and Blaine Cody.

Patience had insisted on coming with him but would not give him a reason.

He had balked but finally given in. It felt good to have her by his side—so cool and refined—and so out of place at the jail.

"Okay, Deputy," Gil said in a tight voice. "I'll put up the bail for my ex-wife."

"What about her boyfriend?" the deputy asked, trying to look as though he didn't recognize him as the D.A.

"No. He can wait for the bail bondsman from Marion to get here in the morning." Gil turned away.

"How much is his bail?" Patience asked, still facing the deputy and looking over Gil's shoulder.

Gil swung back to confront her.

"He needs seven hundred, ten percent." The deputy looked her up and down as though trying to measure her.

"Are the charges that serious?" Patience asked quietly.

"No, but he's got a record. We don't want him to skip." The deputy leaned against the counter, looking even more curious.

"Patience," Gil said close to her ear, "that biker can rot in here for all I care."

"Yes," she whispered back, "but would Darby want him rotting in here?"

"What?" Gil stared at her.

"Darby talks about Blaine a lot," Patience murmured. "He has an affection for him. What if you leave Blaine in jail and Darby finds out..." Her voice faded.

"All right," Gil agreed, guilt tugging at him. He looked to the deputy. "I need to get cash from the ATM machine down the block at the bank entrance."

"No, I'll go and take it out of my account." Patience dug into her bag.

Gil grabbed her elbow as she turned to exit.

"Let me," she said in an undertone. "Blaine might leave you holding the bag. But he won't leave a woman—Darby's teacher—holding it."

He released her. Disgruntled thoughts like furious wasps swooped through his mind.

Within a half hour, Blaine and Coreena walked out into the open area behind the front desk. Both looked disheveled and upset.

"Thanks for coming," Coreena said, pushing her riotous hair back from her makeup-smudged face. Then she saw Patience and stopped.

Patience held out her hand. "I'm Patience Andrews, Darby's—"

"Darby's favorite teacher." Instead, Blaine shook her hand. "I hear you're the one who bailed me out."

"Yes," Patience explained. "I know Darby wouldn't want you to spend the night in jail—"

"Don't worry, lady. I won't skip and leave you holding the bag," Blaine growled. "No matter what the D.A. thinks." The man tossed his head at Gil.

"I didn't think you would," Patience replied, her voice sounding confident.

Coreena eyed her.

Patience offered her a hand again. "And I'm glad to finally meet you, Mrs. Montgomery—"

"After the divorce, I took back my maiden name," Coreena snapped. "I'm Ms. Tucker."

"Nice to meet you, Ms. Tucker." Patience pushed her hand closer to Coreena.

"Well, I just wish we weren't meetin' here," Coreena admitted, flushing, as she shook Patience's hand.

Gil herded them all to the door.

Over an hour later in the after-midnight blackness, Gil walked Patience up to her door.

"You didn't need to get out of the car," she said, her collar turned up. "It's cold—"

"*And* late and I wanted to walk you to the door. So I am." Gil gripped her arm. *I want to, I need to hold you once more. Even if I know it's a bad idea.*

He stepped beside her into the shadow on Mrs. Honeycutt's porch. His arms turned her to him and pulled her close. Her wool coat tickled his nose. "Why did you go with me to the jail?"

"It's terrible to have to deal with bail and…"

Her compassionate reply made him tuck her even closer. He buried his face deeper into the collar of her winter coat.

He expected her to pull away. She didn't.

"Aren't you going to ask me how I know that?" she asked.

"No," Gil said with a serious note of finality. He kissed her mouth. But before he could forget himself and linger too long, he released her. "Good night."

He shuffled down the steps. Halfway down the walk, he heard her close the door behind him and lock it.

About a week later on a Saturday morning, Patience sat on a gray molded-plastic chair outside the door of the county parole office, waiting for her mother to be done with her weekly interview. The office was nestled in one of those antacid-pink corridors in the basement of the courthouse.

Her mother had finally been questioned by the sheriff earlier in the week, a painful experience for both of them. So far, however, no one outside of the sheriff's office had made any sign that they knew that this had happened.

Dear Lord, please keep this from being known. I don't know if I can bear another round of gossip. But if it comes, please help me survive once again.

After checking that she still had the corridor to herself, Patience glanced up at the large institutional wall clock. They had Christmas shopping to do. Mrs. Honeycutt was driving them with her to the Marion Mall and would be picking them up soon. She'd wanted to come later with Bunny, but Bunny had assumed Patience was going with her mother. So what could Patience do?

Hurry up, Mom. I don't want anyone to see me here. No one has found out yet that you are on parole.

Patience tried to keep her hands still in her lap. But one kept slipping up and combing through her bangs.

Stop it.

Patience wondered if the sheriff had contacted her mother's parole officer to tell him that one of his parolee's fingerprints had been found at a crime scene. Coming to the courthouse hadn't bothered her when she'd come with Gil to bail out Blaine. He was not family.

Hurry up, Mother, before someone—

Then what she feared happened…

Her mother stepped out of the office still talking to her parole officer, and down the corridor came the dark-haired juror—what was her name? Harrington? The woman who had let it be known that Patience was the one responsible for the hung jury.

The Harrington woman stopped and gave Patience, her mother and the parole officer a very satisfied double take. "So it's true?" the woman said. "Your own mother is an ex-con? I had to see it for myself."

Chapter Nine

Huge Christmas balls—red, green, gold and frosty white—dangled from the high ceiling of the vast, echoing mall. Branches of artificial greenery draped every shop doorway. Highly artistic faux pine trees helped clog the aisles in front of stores. Christmas carolers, dressed in nineteenth-century garb, roamed the gleaming terrazzo floor. And in the center of the mall, a grinning Santa posed with a pair of howling and protesting toddlers.

An instant connection with them rumbled through Patience. She didn't want to be here. After being seen at the courthouse just an hour ago, she wasn't in the mood to smile for Santa's elf either. *Who had tipped off the Harrington woman that Martina was on parole? How could everything go so terribly wrong?*

"What's the matter, Patience?" Her mother spoke

into her right ear over the voices and noises that echoed around them.

Patience felt her lips tighten even more. They were starting to feel numb. "It's nothing." *It's just that you've been my cross to bear since I was born. And I'm tired of it. I'm sick of you wreaking havoc in my life, shaming me.*

Carolers passed right in front of them joyously singing, "'God rest ye merry gentlemen, let nothing you dismay—'"

Yeah, right. Put a cork in it.

Her conscience bound itself around her lungs like a tourniquet squeezing, bringing her back to herself with a jolt of real pain. *I'm sorry, Lord. I'm sorry. I know what you want me to do, but it's so hard…*

That excused not a thing and she knew it. *Forgive me, Father. Help me. Change my heart. Pour out your love and let it flow through me, so that I have love for her.*

But there will be a new tide of gossip! She shut her mind to the voice that had shrieked this, her own voice, her own frustration and embarrassment.

She fought to control her emotions. *This is all in God's hands. There's nothing I can do.*

"Forgive us our trespasses as we forgive those who trespass against us." Her memory began flowing with verses she'd memorized. "'Love one another as I have loved you. How many times should you forgive?

Seventy times seven. Honor thy mother and father…'''

"Patience," her mother pleaded.

Patience forced a smile. "Let's see if we can find
a lovely wedding present for Cousin Gracie."

Her mother's pinched face relaxed. "Yes, yes. I
wish I'd had a chance to meet her fiancé."

"He's a great guy." Patience wove her mother
through the unpredictable ebb and flow of the shoppers toward a nearby linens shop. "You'll meet him
at the wedding."

"Oh, no." Her mother turned her head away. "I
don't think I'll be able to attend Gracie's wedding."

The tone of her mother's instant refusal and reluctance to look toward Patience revealed her mother's
low self-esteem. The cause of this wasn't hard to
guess. Facing the past, sober now, couldn't be easy.

"Mom, I'm sure you'll be invited." *If you're still
in AA and not in jail again.* Patience cringed at her
own nastiness.

"I've never been much of an aunt to Gracie or her
sister Annie," her mother muttered. "And after I attended Annie's wedding…after what happened…"
Her mother parted from Patience, walking briskly,
overtaking Bunny who'd gotten separated from them
in the holiday crowd.

But her mother's comment had yanked to the surface another horrible memory—Annie's wedding reception, with her mother roaring drunk and having a

humiliating row with her brother, screaming, "I'll never forgive you, Mike! You holier-than-thou hypocrite! You stole my daughter from me!"

In her pale blue bridesmaid dress, Patience—shedding hot tears of shame—had fled from the reception hall. She'd climbed aboard a passing RTA bus crowded with gawking, whispering strangers and gone home to Uncle Mike's house alone. She'd wept so hard that night she'd made herself sick to her stomach. The same sick feeling rose in her stomach now. She braced herself against it.

The mall carolers passed again, now singing, "All is calm, all is bright."

Patience let Bunny and her mother drift farther ahead. She couldn't trust herself to be near either of them. She longed to scream at her mother and recount to Bunny all the disgusting things her mother had ever done in private and in public. *No.*

Patience sank onto a cramped vacant spot on a bench-length of exhausted, bebagged shoppers. A loud cheerful intercom voice announced, "Only six more shopping days till Christmas."

The woman beside Patience groaned. "I'd rather be nine months pregnant and forced to ride a donkey than shop one more day."

Patience couldn't have said it better herself. The Christmas spirit had deserted her and its departure left her thin and flat.

Then she spotted a bookstore directly across from

her with a colorful display of children's books. She rose and let another wilted shopper take her seat. Patience wondered if Darby had a copy of *Mike Mulligan and His Steam Shovel.*

The next morning, Patience forced herself to dress with care in a pale pink wool suit. Her mother had begged off going to church. Patience hadn't tried to persuade her. *I'm going regardless. I won't stay away from church no matter what anyone says.* She swirled on blush and lip gloss, trying to give her strained and pale face reflected in the mirror some life.

Finally outdoors and feeling all alone in this bitterly cold world, she shivered and power walked the deserted blocks to church. Her footsteps made a crunching sound on top of a trace of the powder-dry snow that had fallen overnight.

Inside the half-filled sanctuary, resisting the urge to settle far in the back, she made herself take a seat on her usual pew near the middle. She refused to change her routine, as if she was expecting disapproving stares and avid glances cast at her. *I've endured public humiliation before. I can do it again.*

She stared forward at the pulpit lavishly decorated with balsam branches and holly. The fragrance of pine wafted over her. The advent wreath set on the table in front of the pulpit displayed three lavender candles already burning under glass lamps. Today was the last Advent Sunday. A purple candle lay upon the white linen tablecloth beside the wreath, ready to signal the Christ child would come before the next Sunday.

The organist began playing, "O come, O come, Emanuel and ransom captive Israel." In five days, Christmas would come. This thought brought no consolation. She'd have to spend it here with her mother, far from the family she loved. A lone tear trickled down her cheek. She blinked furiously to dry her eye.

Lord, I wanted to spend Christmas at Uncle Mike's. It would have been so good to spend it with everyone, everyone who loves me. She pictured Uncle Mike's comfortable living room with a large white spruce like the ones he always bought. Then her memory summoned up the sounds of laughter and impromptu caroling as she and her cousins decorated the Christmas tree.

She suppressed a sob that hovered just below the surface. She breathed in and out, calming herself. *I can't show weakness. I can't let anyone see that I am bothered, feeling weak.*

A hopeful thought came to her. Maybe very few people had heard the new gossip yet. After all, it had only been twenty-four hours since that woman had glimpsed her and her mother in the courthouse. But this did little to settle Patience's nerves. She closed her eyes and recited the Lord's Prayer, letting it soothe and strengthen her, too.

A sudden pounding of feet on the carpeted aisle ricocheted around her. "Miss Andrews! Miss Andrews!'' Darby squealed. ''We came to your church today.''

Laying a hand on his shoulder, Patience welcomed Darby whose pink-cheeked face beamed at her.

Gil, with his father breathing down his neck from behind, faced Patience and greeted her. The drawn look she wore cut Gil to the heart. ''Good morning, or should I say, Merry Christmas?''

''Merry Christmas,'' she returned, her lovely though pensive face scanning his.

He took the soft hand she offered him and squeezed it. Her warmth made his chilled hands feel colder. He let go with regret.

''Can we sit with you?'' Darby's voice carried throughout the sanctuary as he bounced on the balls of his feet.

Gil's dad gave a sharp sound of displeasure.

Gil ignored it, waiting for Patience's reply.

She studied Gil as though weighing his motives.

''If you don't mind,'' he murmured. *That's why we came.*

''No. No.'' She moved farther along the pew, making room for him and his dad.

His father reached around Gil and grasped Darby's shoulder. ''This young man,'' he said in a harsh voice, ''better sit between you and me, so we can make sure he behaves.''

Resentment spurted inside Gil. He gripped his father's rough arthritic hand on Darby's shoulder, restraining him. "That's okay, Captain. Darby can sit where he wants."

Patience watched this, but voiced no comment.

His father flashed him an irate glare, but released Darby.

"I want to sit by my teacher."

Smiling, Patience held out a hand to Darby.

Grinning, Darby scrambled up on the seat beside Patience while Gil and his father sat down on Darby's other side.

The Captain's displeasure radiated like hot sparks around Gil.

"What's that?" Darby pointed toward the Advent wreath.

Patience explained it and told Darby to watch for the last candle to be lit during the service.

In Gil's ear, his father growled, "I hope you're going to make the boy behave himself. He needs to learn to be quiet here. This isn't a playground."

Gil nodded, but did not trust himself to say more. How many times had he suffered through church under his father's rigid discipline and disapproving glare?

Why did he insist on coming with us this morning? He never attends church. I shouldn't have let it drop that we were going to services when he called at breakfast. I should have known better.

Patience was now showing Darby the attendance card and small pencils on the back of the pew in front of them. Placing a card on top of a hymnal, she was having Darby print his name on it.

It had been a scramble getting here today. But his fears that Darby might cause a disturbance in church ebbed.

Last night, Gil had received a call from a juror from Dan Putnam's trial asking him if he knew that Patience Andrews's mother was on parole. He'd gritted his teeth and given a noncommittal reply. But the news that others had discovered the truth about Patience's mother had impelled him to make the effort to get Darby up and into his suit for church. Perhaps, his being seen, sitting beside Patience in church, would dampen the gossip about her mother being an ex-con.

Certainly, this was what had prompted him to come, nothing less than that could have forced him to appear in this church where he hadn't felt welcome for many years—firstly, after his "outlaw" marriage, and more so, after his unwanted divorce. He'd been the prodigal son who'd married the woman everyone thought beneath him and then in the end, she'd divorced him.

And no doubt everyone in the quickly filling pews around them would have heard by now about Coreena being arrested last weekend in a melee at that bar at the edge of town. *If anyone says anything to me about that in front of Darby...*

But the service unfolded without a hitch. Darby sat

beside Patience and turned to her occasionally for explanation as if she were on duty as his teacher to explain church to him.

His son's eager curiosity didn't bother Gil. In fact, it made him regret that he'd not brought Darby to a church service since the day he had been christened as a baby. Still, Gil sensed his father's mounting restless displeasure. The Captain barked the responsive reading, his critical gaze never leaving Darby.

Gil kept his focus on Patience and his son while she concentrated her attention on Darby. But did she sense his father's growing censure?

Gil's muscles tightened till he felt like a stick figure, but he didn't betray this by so much as a glance toward the Captain.

Finally, the organist struck up the postlude, "Joy to the world, the Lord is come. Let earth receive her King." Gil rose and caught Darby as he leaped into his arms with an exuberant shout.

"Darby," the Captain scowled and scolded, "don't yell in church."

Darby turned a puzzled expression toward his grandfather.

"He didn't yell—" Gil began.

"It's the time he spends with that worthless mother of his." The Captain's words poured out like infection from a wound. "He's her son all right. I warned you about bad blood—"

"My mommy doesn't have bad blood." Darby stuck out his lower lip.

"This is an adult conversation," the Captain snapped. "Children should speak when spoken to."

"Leave him alone," Gil warned his dad in an undertone as he urged him into the aisle. *Let's get out of here before we make a scene. That's the last thing Patience or I need.*

"My mommy doesn't have bad blood," Darby insisted, his face scrunched up with indignation.

His grandfather turned away and stalked up the aisle.

"My mommy doesn't have bad blood!" Darby yelled after him.

That evening, ahead through the late-December night, Patience glimpsed the front-porch light glowing on Gil's ranch home. Hugging the shadows, she'd walked all the way to Gil's house, almost two miles from Bunny's through an unexpected wet snowfall.

This morning's scene at church had haunted her all day. She had to do something to help distract Darby from his grandfather's name-calling. The Captain's cruel words in church had turned every ear within hearing distance toward them. He'd humiliated his son and grandson in public. *I know how that feels.*

Icy wind whipped around her as she reached the front door. Standing in the shadows away from the coach light, she waited for Gil to answer the doorbell that she could hear trilling through the house.

She stamped her feet and admitted she'd put off buying new snow boots too long. Melting snow had seeped into her heavy socks. She shuddered with cold.

The door opened. Gil gawked at her. "Patience?"

"May I come in?" She shivered again.

"You must be frozen." He stepped back and ushered her inside. "What are you doing out on a night like this? Who dropped you off?"

"I walked." *My feet are freezing.* She bent and began tugging off her sodden boots on the entryway rug. Keeping her head bent gave her an excuse to resist looking at him.

"Walked? In this mess?"

"I wanted to give Darby his Christmas present early." *And I had to see you again.*

"You should have called," Gil continued scolding. "I'd have been glad to come and pick you up."

"I'm used to walking." Her last boot released her foot and she stared down at her sopping-wet and frigid socks, still avoiding eye contact with this man who could move her like no other.

"Take those socks off, too." He left her and jogged down the hall toward his room. "I'll get you a pair of mine to wear. We'll put those in the dryer."

"I hate to put you out like this," she called after him.

Darby stepped out of his room, and into the hall. "Who's here? Mommy?"

''No, it's Miss Andrews,'' Gil replied as he entered his bedroom.

Darby brightened and raced down to her. ''Miss Andrews! Hi!''

''Good evening, Darby.''

Hearing her warm welcome to his son melted some of the lingering pain—a stiffness, an ache—from the scene this morning at church. Gil snatched a pair of socks from the fresh laundry in a basket on his bed and hurried back down the hall to his son.

''Yesterday, we finally got our tree up,'' Darby informed her. ''Look.''

Patience looked through the doorway to the living room. ''It's a big one. You did a great job decorating it.''

''What's that in the bag?'' Darby asked, his gaze fixed on the cloth bag over her arm.

The tip of a thin but wide package, wrapped in green foil, peeped out of the top. ''It's an early Christmas present for you. But, Darby, you mustn't mention this at school. I don't want the other students to think I'm playing favorites. They might not understand that you, your dad and I are friends. See what I mean?''

''We're friends?'' Darby marveled.

''Of course we are.'' Gil reached Patience and offered her a pair of his white sport socks. ''But you still need to obey Miss Andrews at school—''

''*I know that,*'' Darby said, loudly and clearly insulted.

"I thought you would." Patience sat down on a chair at the edge of the living room and slipped on the too-big socks.

Gil watched her every move.

"That feels better. Thanks." She sighed.

The sigh whistled its way through him.

Baby-vulture-like, Darby hung over her shoulder as close as he could without touching the package. "What'd you bring me?"

Gil wondered the same thing.

She slipped the gift out and handed it to him. "Go ahead. Open it."

With gusto, Darby ripped open the foil wrapping paper. "A book!"

"Yes, one of my favorites." Patience stroked the book's slender spine.

"Mine, too," Gil said, glancing at the black, red and white cover. Just the kind of book Darby loved. It had a machine on it.

"I hope I didn't buy a book he already has." Patience looked worried.

"No, no," Gil said, hurrying to reassure her. "I didn't even remember this story until I saw it right now."

"Read it to me." Darby pushed the book into her hands and then scurried over to the sofa. "Sit here beside me." He patted the couch cushion.

Patience chuckled. Padding silently over the carpet in Gil's white socks, she sat down next to Darby.

Gil sat down on his son's other side. Her coming tonight was a gift in itself.

Patience pointed to the book's cover. "Let's sound out the title, shall we?"

"Okay. Mmm-ike," Darby started.

"Right. Now." Patience pointed to the second word of the title.

"Mmmm-uuu-li-gun."

"Right. Mike Mulligan," Patience repeated. "Great. And now what has Mike got?"

"A...st...st..." Darby paused.

"Eem," Gil prompted.

"Steam," Darby repeated.

"Well done," Patience murmured.

"Sh...sh...ooo...vellll," Darby finished.

"Great. *Mike Mulligan and His Steam Shovel*. A classic."

"You read it now, okay?" Darby pushed the book toward her, rocking with excitement.

She glanced at Gil with a question on her face.

"Yes, you read it to us, Teacher," he said with a grin. He longed to slip his arm around her and gather her close, the three of them together. Like a real family?

She opened the book and began reading.

He barely heard the words. Her voice, that rich voice that wrapped itself around his nerves like black velvet held sway over him. He drew closer to her, not wanting to miss a syllable that purred from deep inside her throat.

She's doing it again. She's caring for Darby. No wonder I can't help myself. I try to keep her from my mind, Lord. But she keeps slipping under my defenses. She's filled with love and it overflows from her. But how can it be? I know the truth about her awful childhood. How did she become a loving woman like this?

As he looked over her shoulder down at the book, he watched her face as she read, resisting the urge to stroke her pale cheek. *I can't give in to the temptation.*

It was a tough battle. But by the time she read, "The End," Gil had pulled his self-control together. "What do you say, Darby?" he prompted.

"Thanks for the book and for reading me the story." Darby hugged the new book to his chest. "I'm going to bring this to school."

"Perhaps it would be better if you kept the book in your room." Patience stroked Darby's dark waves. "You might forget and tell a classmate that I gave it to you. Remember, they don't need to know we are friends away from school."

"Okay," Darby agreed. "I won't forget. Promise."

"Time for bed, pal." Gil ruffled his hair. "Say good-night to Miss Andrews."

"I'll be going then." Patience rose, obviously ready to bolt.

"You will not." Gil touched her elbow. *I can't let*

you go yet. "I'm going to get this guy to bed and then we'll share a cup of coffee before I drive you home. My neighbor, a grandmother herself, always helps me out by coming over when I have a quick errand to run. Relax." He didn't wait for a reply, but left her curled up on his couch.

Within minutes, he returned to the living room. "Why don't we go into the kitchen." She padded behind him until he waved her forward through the hall to the kitchen. Soon he had the coffeemaker gurgling and brewing decaf caramel-vanilla coffee. The three aromas filled the kitchen. But Patience distracted him more.

He sat near her chair at the table as he had so recently on the night they'd ended up at the county jail. It might fit her mother but not her. "Thank you again."

"What for?" she asked, her head tilted slightly.

"For caring about my son."

She cast her eyes downward. "He's an easy little guy to care about."

"His kindergarten teacher and Sunday-school teacher don't share your assessment."

"That's unfortunate," she murmured, still not meeting his gaze.

The coffeemaker hissed to a finish and he rose to fill two mugs. From the fridge, he brought half-and-half to the table and then the mugs. He sat again, reining in his attraction to this woman. "I was in the room when the sheriff questioned your mother."

"She told me her fingerprints were there because she had gone upstairs to get something Mrs. Carmichael asked her to get," Patience inserted, stirring cream into the coffee.

"Yes, and when we talked to Mrs. Carmichael, she remembered asking your mother to get her inhaler from the drawer in her bedroom." He poured a generous shot of cream into his coffee, too. The creamy white disappeared and then swirled the dark brown into tan.

"So, suspecting and questioning my mother was just a waste of time," Patience said in a starched tone.

"In a majority of cases, most leads are a waste of time, but we have to follow up each of them no matter what." He took a cautious sip of the hot brew.

"I know," she admitted. "What about the other pair of prints?"

"We still haven't identified them." He watched her, admired her over the rim of his mug.

For a few moments, they sipped coffee in silence, the topic of the fingerprints finished.

As the silence stretched, he noticed everything about her—a small scar on her forehead half hidden by her hair, a dainty mole beside her lower lip.… *Stop noticing.* He couldn't.

She sipped her coffee, staring into her mug. "If you

were going by past record, you might have wanted my prints.''

He started to object.

''You already know about my mother's problems. Well, because of them, I had my troubles with the law as a child. I started running away when I was thirteen,'' she went on as though he weren't there, not looking at him.

He sat back in his chair.

''I didn't run away far or for long, just when my mom's drinking made it unsafe for me to be at home. I usually took refuge at my uncle Mike's house.''

''Why didn't he try to get custody of you?'' Gil asked, hating to hear what she'd suffered.

''He did in the end, when my mom married again. I was fifteen and couldn't face two alcoholic parents. I ran away for real. This time I left Chicago. It took Uncle Mike two weeks to find me…on the streets of St. Louis.''

''Anything could have happened to you.'' Gil couldn't conceal his shock. *Anything!*

''Well, the angels were watching over me, and except for my being incredibly dirty and starving, I was unscathed.''

''We all do stupid things when we're young.'' *I married Coreena Tucker, the most notorious girl in town, believing everyone was just prejudiced against her.*

But all he said was, ''So you went to live with your uncle?''

"Yes, he is a wonderful man. Everything I am or hope to be is due to Aunt Mary and Uncle Mike. If not for their love and care, I'd probably have followed my mother's example. But they taught me about love and God and I decided to take a different path." Her face glowed with emotion, with love for her uncle.

"You're a wonderful person." He felt an incredible joy to be able to say this to her at last. "You've done more for my son—"

"Why did your dad act like that this morning?" she said, deflecting his praise. *She won't even let me thank her.*

"Being a retired captain, my father insists on proper decorum and discipline." He grimaced. "Sometimes I wonder if I should let him spend as much time with Darby as I do. But I..."

She put a slender hand over his. "Darby loves his grandfather. He speaks of him with affection."

Gil had trouble breathing. He turned his palm upward and captured her hand, kept it.

With her thumb, she traced a pattern on the mound of sensitive flesh beneath his thumb. "But it's obvious that your father didn't approve of your marriage."

Her soft touch ensnared him and he concentrated on the motion of her delicate fingertips. "He hated my marrying Coreena. He hated Coreena, wouldn't accept her at all. My mom was caught in the middle between us."

She shook her head with what appeared to be sincere understanding. "You're going to have to confront him about criticizing her in front of Darby. Your son loves his mother and he won't turn against her. He'll turn against your father."

The phone rang.

Gil burned with aggravation. He would never bring Patience into his kitchen again and he'd make sure to unplug the phone whenever she visited. He snatched the phone off the wall. "Yes," he snarled.

Chapter Ten

Gil's harsh tone shocked Patience and shattered the mood. Their intimate conversation had deepened her awareness of him, had drawn them together. But now he was handing her the receiver and looking thunderous.

Wondering what the crisis was, she took it, and with reluctance held it next to her face. "Hello?"

"Patience, I'm so sorry to interrupt," Bunny apologized, "but a Mr. Pulaski called and wants you to call him right back. It's important, very important he said."

Patience's hand holding the phone shook. "Thanks, Bunny, I'll call him as soon as I get home."

"He's not at home. He gave me this number—it's to a Chicago police station." Bunny repeated the number and Patience memorized it.

"Okay, thanks, I'll head home right now." Patience hung up after goodbyes. "I have to leave."

Gil clutched her by the arms. "No, what's going on?"

"Gil, I..." *Should I tell him or not?*

"I'm not letting you go until you tell me what's happened. Patience, I'm on your side. Don't you know that by now?"

His declaration made her decision easy. "I need to make a long-distance call to Chicago."

"About what?"

"Just trust me. I'll pay you for the call—"

He made a sound of disgust. "I can afford a phone call. Go ahead."

Patience quickly dialed the number and almost immediately was answered by a brusque voice telling her she'd reached such and such Chicago precinct. "This is Patience Andrews. May I speak to Mr. Pulaski, please? I'm returning his call."

A pause and then she heard Mr. Pulaski's robust voice in her ear. "Patience! We finally hit pay dirt!"

"What? You found—"

"We found three items that matched the Perkins theft report."

"Where?" Patience could hardly draw breath.

Gil stared at her, his expression both curious and impatient.

"Gil," she whispered and held up one finger, asking for his silence.

"A raid on a warehouse here," Mr. Pulaski said, forcing her back to silence. "Suspected drugs, but the officers also found out it was a high-class fencing operation, too. They gave me a call when they discovered that a few antique items matched the list I'd given them. Then they checked on the official theft report that had been forwarded to their computer system. They're dusting the antiques for prints as we speak."

"Oh, Mr. Pulaski, you don't know what this means to me and to Dan Putnam. This shows that someone else must have or at least could have taken the stolen items and gotten them out of the county while Dan was already in custody." Tears moistened her eyes. "Here, I'd like you to tell this to Gil Montgomery, Cole County district attorney." She handed Gil the phone. "It's Mr. Pulaski, a friend in Chicago. He's a retired Chicago cop and he has some information for you about the Putnam case."

Patience sank back into her chair. She felt herself glowing like Christmas lights on the tree, shimmering with joy. *Thank you, Father. You've answered my prayers. They'll have to let Dan Putnam go now.*

She glanced up at Gil, who gripped the receiver. He looked as though someone had hit him in the face with a wet sock. He was muttering, "Yes…yes…I see."

Gil, be happy about this. Don't spoil it for me. She pressed her folded hands to her lips.

''Thank you, sir,'' Gil said, sounding very stiff, very professional. ''Please extend my gratitude to the officers who made the bust. This will certainly make some difference in the case. The sheriff will need to be advised of this new evidence. Thank you again.'' Then he handed her the phone.

She gazed into his eyes, willing him to understand why she'd taken this action, and accept this information for what it was. ''Thank you, Mr. Pulaski,'' she said into the receiver. ''You're wonderful.''

''My pleasure.'' The ex-cop's voice pulsed with glee. ''It gives me a good feeling. Yes, it does. I don't think a man can retire from law enforcement completely. Still like to turn up that important piece of evidence. It's a real high. Thanks, Patience. You've given me a great Christmas present.''

Patience tried to thank him again, but he chuckled and hung up with ''Merry Christmas!'' Patience replaced the receiver on the wall. He slumped back into his chair near her and stared at her, the corners of his mouth stiff. ''Explain this to me.''

She did, starting with her initial call to Mr. Pulaski and how she knew him from Chicago and why she'd contacted him. All the while, she watched for some easing up in Gil's posture, some indication he believed her now.

He listened without interrupting her and without giving any sign of what was going on in his head.

She finally drew to a close, her pulse still racing.

What would he say? Would he be able to refute this new evidence?

"I can't believe it," Gil said flatly.

Her face fell, her lungs contracted. "But…"

He lowered his head into his hands. "I can't believe it."

She flushed hot. "Why? Because you didn't find this evidence?"

He looked up at her. "No, not that." He took her hands in his.

She tugged, but he wouldn't release her.

"It's just…I was so sure…"

"So sure I was wrong?" Her voice throbbed in her throat.

"No, so sure I was right about Dan's motive." He gripped her hands together. "It's hard to admit I might be mistaken. The finding of this evidence will make a difference, but how much I can't tell. Yet."

She finally wrenched her hands free. "You still don't have any hard evidence against Dan. And this find may lead to someone else."

He rubbed his forehead as if it pained him. "I don't know if this information will be enough to free Dan—"

"Why not?" she challenged him.

He heaved a sigh. "First of all, we have to find out how the antiques got to that Chicago warehouse. We need to eliminate the possibility that somehow Putnam could have handed them off to someone before he was arrested.''

Patience viewed Gil with a sour taste in her mouth. *So you'll fight against Dan to the end. You don't admit defeat easily, do you, District Attorney Montgomery?* She rose. ''I'll be leaving now.'' Her cool voice glinted with ice, chilling her from the inside. She brushed past him heading for the hallway to get her boots and coat.

''No you don't.'' He pursued her down the hall. ''I'm driving you home.''

By the front door, they had a brief tug-of-war over her boots. She finally let go. The boots thumped back down onto the quarry-tile entryway. ''What's wrong with you?''

''I'm sorry.'' Gil sucked in air. ''You're taking my words wrong.''

''How so?'' She gave him an imperious look and folded her arms. She was breathing fast herself.

''I don't doubt that Mr. Pulaski's information will make a big change in the case against Dan Putnam.''

She wouldn't meet his eyes. ''I can't see why you can't see that Dan's a victim of prejudice—''

''Please. This is my job.'' He lifted her chin with his forefinger.

She permitted herself a look at him.

''I don't walk into your classroom,'' he continued, ''and tell you how to teach. There are certain procedures I must follow in the course of my job.''

"I don't think Dan Putnam ought to spend Christmas in jail." She huffed.

"If I agree to try to get everything wound up before then, will you let me drive you home?" His voice coaxed her, apologized beyond the words.

She stared at him hard. "Deal." She held out her hand.

He shook it.

As always, his touch softened her, drew her to him. *Lord, what's happening between us?*

The next morning at 9:01 a.m., Gil sat across the desk from Vincent Caruthers in the small office at the back of his Shop on the Square. The sheriff had had to appear in court this morning and had asked Gil to question Caruthers. The scent of lemon oil hung over them, too strong for an early appointment. But he and the sheriff needed information and Caruthers might have it. Gil tried to breathe through his mouth.

"What can I do for you, Montgomery?" Caruthers asked.

Gil tried to read the man's expression but came up without a clue. Either Caruthers had a lot on his mind or nothing at all. "We received some valuable information last night on the Putnam case."

"Oh?" Caruthers sounded uninterested but polite.

"Three of the items stolen from Mrs. Perkins have turned up in a Chicago warehouse." Gil extracted a sheet of paper from the briefcase at his feet. "This is a copy of the fax Sheriff Longworthy received from the Chicago Police Department last night.''

His lips puckered, Caruthers accepted the sheet and perused it. Then he opened a file drawer to the right of his desk and pulled out a single paper from a folder. He laid the papers side by side on his desk and scanned them, making little wheezes and tsks. ''Yes, you're right. These three do match items I appraised for Mrs. Perkins. They are especially fine pieces and worth quite a pretty penny. A Minton teapot, a Lalique vase and a very small Tiffany lamp. Yes, yes. Choice pieces.''

Gil retrieved the fax sheet and tucked it away. ''I need your help then.''

''In what way?'' Caruthers looked at him almost without curiosity.

What gives? Everyone in town is interested in this case. Why aren't you? Gil slid back in the roomy chair. ''Putnam was arrested in his home less than an hour after his mother had been attacked. We're trying to figure out if he—on his way between the two houses—could have handed off these items and others to a third party before being arrested.''

Caruthers raised a palm as if to say, ''Who knows?''

''Do you know of anyone in the area who would receive such items?''

''You mean like me?'' Caruthers's tone had stiffened.

''No,'' Gil said, placating. ''You are not under sus-

picion. I just thought that since you've been in business in this area for over thirty years, you might know
if someone…''

Caruthers stared at him. ''No, I don't know of any
of my colleagues in this area that have that kind of
reputation.''

Gil gritted his teeth. A dead end or not? ''So you're
saying that the likelihood of Putnam being able to
hand off—''

''Let me give you some information that might be
of help.''

''That's what I'm here for.'' Gil bent his head
slightly forward, ceding Caruthers the floor.

''There are theft rings that move around the country
picking up antiques. Just as the local authorities become aware of their activities, they are usually already
out of town.''

''Really?'' Gil raised an eyebrow. ''The money for
antiques is that good?''

''These rings are very small and very few but very
efficient.'' Caruthers sounded grim.

''How do they know what houses to target?'' Gil
asked, leaning his elbows on the arms of his chair.

''In the past, they would judge a book by its cover
or I mean, a house by its appearance.'' Caruthers
smoothed his pencil-thin mustache. ''Usually large
old Victorians—whether run-down or newly refur-
bished—make good targets as repositories of antiques.

But the Internet has brought a whole new way for these rings to locate items they are interested in.''

''The Internet?'' Gil's tone gave voice to his skepticism. ''What's that got to do with antiques?''

''There are dozens of auction sites on the Internet.'' Caruthers waved at the computer on an adjacent desk. ''Well e-bay is the most well known, but many more exist. Also, there are appraisal Web sites where professionals like myself can post items and check that appraisals are accurate by comparing items.''

Gil steepled his fingers in front of his chin. ''Did you use any of these sites for Mrs. Perkins's antiques?''

''I did. She had a few more valuable and some rarer pieces and I wanted to be sure I wasn't offering more than the trade would allow.''

''Was that wise?'' Gil made direct eye contact with the dealer.

Caruthers shrugged. ''I hope it wasn't unwise.'' Caruthers sounded unconcerned. ''I didn't think at the time that I was exposing Mrs. Perkins to robbery and assault, I can assure you. I've known her for many years and have sold her and her late husband many items in the past.''

''But could a theft ring have found out where the items were?''

Caruthers gave a grudging nod. ''The Internet sites are supposed to be secure, but hackers… I really don't know anything about that end of it, but I suppose some people know enough to find out anything they would want about someone who posts on these sites.

"This is a small town," Caruthers continued. "It wouldn't be difficult for someone to come through town and start talking to people and to find out where some of the items I listed could be found. They might even have stopped in at my shop. Often, these operators already have a buyer or receiver for the goods they are looking to steal."

Gil stared at the dealer. "Did you post anything for Mrs. Carmichael?"

"No. No," Caruthers hurried to reassure him. "I haven't done any appraisals for her at all. But it's common knowledge that her house is decorated with antiques, family heirlooms."

"Can you think of anything else that might help us out in this investigation?" Gil rose, his head buzzing with new possibilities.

"I'll spend some time thinking about it and let you know." He offered Gil his soft, pampered hand perfunctorily. "Does this mean that Dan Putnam will be released soon?"

"If not completely exonerated, he will probably be released on bail before Christmas." *I promised Patience. And I better keep that pledge.* "I don't think he presents a flight risk anymore—"

"And the second robbery and this fax put his guilt in doubt?" Caruthers asked, not looking or sounding very involved.

"So it seems." Gil turned to leave.

Caruthers followed him.

As Gil passed one of the gleaming, spotless glass-topped counters, he halted. Something small and dainty had caught his eye. He stared down at it.

"Did you see something?"

"Yes, how much…I'd like to see that." Gil pointed at the far right of the display.

"A very fine piece." Caruthers's tone warmed. "It will just take me a minute…."

Three days later on a cold and blustery Christmas Eve, Gil rang the doorbell at Bunny Honeycutt's. Within minutes, Bunny threw the door wide open, spilling light onto the darkened porch. "Come in. Come in. Merry Christmas."

He handed her a well-wrapped bouquet of red roses. "Merry Christmas."

"You dear man. Red roses at Christmas. How deliciously decadent. Come in and get warm by the fire. Dinner's almost ready."

The fragrances of sage dressing and pumpkin pie enveloped him as he obeyed his hostess. His glasses fogged up and he took them off and wiped them with a handkerchief.

Bunny hurried away, saying she had to get out a vase for the flowers.

Gil shed his wool coat and scarf on the already crowded hall tree and stepped into the living room across the hall. Only candles, the hearth fire and a brightly lit Christmas tree gave out light in the cozy room. Bunny had invited him, he was sure, because she knew from his dad that he'd be alone on Christmas Eve. He'd come in spite of his dad's presence, craving a few moments alone with Patience. To see her, he would suffer his father's displeasure.

"Merry Christmas."

Gil recognized Martina's rough voice and looked toward her where she sat, thin and pale, in a wing chair beside the fire. "Same to you."

"Yes, Merry Christmas," Dottie said in her funny breathy voice.

He wished her the same, and then at last faced his father who sat beside Dottie on the sofa. "Merry Christmas, Captain." Would his father reply or ignore him? They hadn't spoken since their flare-up on Sunday over Coreena.

"Season's greetings, son."

Gil drew a breath of relief. He hadn't wanted their falling-out to spoil the holiday evening for Bunny and her guests.

Patience walked into the room and all the breath rushed out of him. She was wearing an off-white dress of some clingy material that skimmed her figure. Small gold hoops dangled from her ears and her face glowed with a blush—from his attention? "You look great," he said.

From the sofa, Dottie giggled.

"You dressed up, too. Very nice," Patience said. "Merry Christmas."

If no one had been present, he would have taken her into his arms and persuaded her to stay there. The belief that he could do this, that this was what he wanted more than anything, rolled through him with a silent roar.

Unaware of his marked reaction, she strolled toward him with a dish of fragrantly spiced gingerbread cookies in her hand. "Bunny asked me to start these around. She and my mother baked them yesterday." Tantalizingly near, she held the dish out to him.

With numb fingers, he lifted a gingerbread man. "Thanks." And the small gift-wrapped box in his pocket niggled at him. When would they have a moment alone?

"You'll have to take some home for Darby," she said and then moved toward his father and Dottie.

"I was hoping you'd be bringing the little dear tonight," Dottie gushed.

"No, he's with his mother tonight," Gil said, not looking at Dottie. "I'll pick him up midmorning tomorrow."

"That's the way with these broken marriages," his dad said gruffly. "The kids pay for their parents' mistakes."

Hot lava scalded Gil's empty stomach. The spicy-cinnamony gingerbread in his mouth turned bitter, galling. *So it's going to be a night of sniping.*

"All parents make mistakes, divorced or not." Martina's voice was low and sad.

Gil turned to her, grateful for her understanding. Her expression was closed but downhearted. *Yes, you must have many regrets.*

"Some parents don't make the mistakes that *others* do," his dad replied with a sharp glance at Martina.

Martina's pale face turned brick red.

Gil looked directly at his father, ashamed of the cheap shot he'd just taken at Martina. Evidently, the Captain had discovered that Martina was a recovering alcoholic.

Patience had frozen halfway to her mother with the cookie dish held out in front of her.

Gil wished to let everyone know that his dad hadn't been the perfect father, either. Gil reached toward Patience and took the dish from her. He set it on the coffee table. "At least I'm in the same town as my son for Christmas. I'm not off—"

"What did Darby want for Christmas?" Patience interrupted in a forced lively tone and then walked to the love seat in the shadows away from the fire.

Thank you, Patience… You're right, this is Christmas. Again, Gil wanted to take Patience's hands in his and leave this room, which was too full of his father's disapproving face and Dottie's flirtatious expression.

Gil glanced around, trying to decide where to sit, somewhere he wouldn't have to look at the Captain.

"Darby wanted a remote-control motorcycle, a Harley—"

"Just like that woman's good-for-nothing boyfriend," his father muttered, just loud enough to be heard.

Gil steeled himself and went on, "Coreena and I decided she should give him the gift he wanted most." Gil realized that his relationship with his ex had improved over the past few months. How? What had changed this? Was it Patience? She was the only new element. "It was her turn. I'm giving him an intricate Lego set. He plays with them the most." ·

"I'm sure he'll enjoy that." Patience motioned to him, inviting him to sit beside her on the love seat.

Gil wondered if she was doing it out of sympathy, since his father had made his agenda for the evening very clear. It must be "Get Gil night." So he didn't argue. He sat down on the love seat, only inches separating them. The scent from the pine tree mingled with Patience's fragrance and heightened all his senses.

Was she responsible for the improvement in the way Coreena was behaving? Had Patience's advice about letting Darby have more access to his mother paid off in easier communication and less resentment? Gil glanced at Patience. The light from the fire gilded her blond hair.

She leaned closer to him. "Thanks for getting Dan

Putnam out of jail this morning.'' She gave him a private look.

Bunny bustled into the room, a cut-glass vase with his roses held out in front of her. ''I'm going to put the flowers in the window so everyone who passes can enjoy them, too.''

''They're lovely,'' Patience said.

You're lovely. Gil couldn't take his gaze from her.

''Gil, did you see the gorgeous pink poinsettia your father brought tonight?'' Bunny nodded toward the glowing hearth. ''I put it by the fire so it would stay nice and warm.''

''Ah, yeah, it looks great,'' Gil mumbled and glanced at his father, who was giving him a nasty look. Gil's irritation flared again. *Now what did I do? Do roses trump a pink poinsettia?*

Patience rested her hand on the love seat between them.

Was this an offer of understanding? Did she realize his father was needling him? In the flickering shadows cast by the fire, he ventured to lay his hand over hers. He waited for her to withdraw her hand. She didn't.

He curled his fingers around hers. *Don't let her touch be motivated by sympathy about the Captain, Lord. Patience, I want—*

She gave a little sigh only he could hear.

''That meal sure smells wonderful,'' the Captain said, beaming at Bunny.

"Only a few more minutes." Bunny sat down in a chair at an angle to the Captain and Dottie.

"With your long naval career, I'm sure you had to spend many Christmases away from your family, Captain," Bunny said. "What was the most unusual place you ever spent Christmas?"

His father grinned, looking pleased at the subtle compliment implicit in the question.

Gil bristled. His dad had the nerve to mock him because tonight Darby was with his ex-wife. But at least Gil was in the same town as his son on Christmas.

"Well, I guess—" his dad started, grinning at Bunny.

"His most unusual Christmas was spent in Rushton," Gil interrupted with a snap to his voice. "He was only home one Christmas the whole seventeen years we lived here. That's pretty unusual, wouldn't you say?"

The grin on the Captain's face became a scowl.

Dottie giggled nervously.

Chapter Eleven

Later, in Bunny's country kitchen, Patience and Gil both stood with large white dishcloths in hand. He faced her, but she had turned halfway from him, avoiding eye contact. They were both drying the last of the dinner dishes and then the large pots and pans. During the homey, intimate chore, he had successfully hidden his awareness of her every move, every expression, every sound. But his throat had tightened painfully and so had his chest. *How can I make her listen?*

"Well, that's the last." Patience let out a whistling sigh and laid the black enamel roasting pan on the counter. "It's amazing how much time we spend preparing and cleaning up for a dinner that only lasts an hour or so."

He nodded. All the light in the kitchen seemed to

hover over and around the lovely woman before him. He didn't want to talk about dishes. He wanted to talk to Patience alone, had to talk to her—and it had to be alone.

After twitching the damp dishcloth from his hands, she folded it along with hers and hung it over the drying rack. Then she motioned toward the door to the hall. "Shall we join the others?" she asked.

He'd suffered sitting stiffly across from the disapproving Captain throughout dinner. Now Gil had no intention of getting anywhere near his father again tonight.

Could he whisk Patience away to his place? The wind with ice prickles buffeted the kitchen windows, dousing this idea. He shifted on his feet. "I've never seen your place."

"Oh, all right." Patience sounded less than eager. "This way."

She led him to and up a staircase in the chilly back hall. At the top of the back stairs, she unlocked the door and stepped inside, switching on an overhead light fixture.

He entered a small kitchen that opened on to a large room. Before she could prevent him, he walked through the kitchen into the living room. His mouth had gone dry and his throat still felt squeezed tight.

"This is nice." He could have thumped his skull like a ripe watermelon. *You're a conversational genius, Montgomery.*

"I like it." Hanging back as if ready to take him back downstairs, she stood with her hands folded in front of her.

Come up with something fast or it's return to the Captain. "What do these doors lead to?" Gil pointed.

"I have a bedroom and bath. All that I need." Patience stepped back toward the kitchen. Soon she'd be ushering him out.

He grabbed at straws. "Does your mom live up here with you?"

"No, she rents a room downstairs from Bunny by the week." Patience took another retreating step.

Honesty is the best policy. He faced her. "Do we have to go back down right away? I'm kind of hoping they won't miss us and my dad will leave before I do." *And I'll have time to tell you what I need to say, no matter your reaction.*

She nibbled her lower lip. "All right.... Have a seat."

They sat down on a slightly worn sofa, both of them stiff and over two feet apart. Why did it feel as if they were strangers on a first date? Was it because he'd trespassed on this, her private space? Or maybe because he wanted this to be a date?

"I'm sorry," she said, "that your father and you are having—"

"It's nothing new," Gil cut her off, his temper rearing up hotter than before. "We've never gotten along. When I was a kid and he was on active duty, he'd come home from whatever assignment for a few weeks or months. He'd always march into the house, barking orders and evaluating our performance levels, upsetting our peace.''

''Your mom and you?'' Not looking up, she pleated her skirt hem.

He nodded. ''When I was very little, I always looked forward to his homecomings. But by the time I was in fourth grade, I'd learned better. It created a terrible conflict in me. I wanted to see him, and I never wanted to see him again.''

''I know that feeling.'' She rubbed her palms together.

I'll bet you do. ''Anyway, I don't think the Captain and I will ever be close. Nothing I've ever done has been good enough to suit him and quite frankly, I don't try anymore.''

''He cares for Darby.'' Patience settled back against the sofa cushion.

''Yes, but what else does he have left in his life?'' Gil took her cue and stretched out his legs, trying to appear relaxed. ''His career is finished, his wife is dead and he has no hobbies. I really didn't want him to settle here. I told him he shouldn't, that he'd probably be happier somewhere with more activity.''

''Maybe he finally wanted a family.'' Patience angled her body, facing him.

She was so near and approachable.

''Maybe he waited too long.'' He captured her

hand, edging closer to her. "I don't want to talk about my father anymore. I've wasted enough energy on him tonight already." Afraid of losing his nerve, he brought her hand up to his lips and kissed her palm. "I'd rather talk about us."

She made no answer, save a quick intake of breath.

Her response gave him courage. "I know you may not want to hear what I have to say, but I can't hold the words in any longer."

She tried to pull back her hand. "Gil, no, I—"

"I care for you." Taking pains not to hurt her, he imprisoned her hand between both of his. "I think I'm falling in love with you."

Silence except for a swell of girlish laughter from the room below. *Dottie.*

"Gil..." Patience stammered, "I...I'm very flattered, but I'm not..."

"Not what? Not available? Is there someone else in Chicago maybe?" He drew her hand up to his cheek.

"No, no one anywhere and there won't be." She shook her head, looking downhearted. "You know all about me, about how I was raised. I'm just not a good candidate to fall in love with. I come with...with baggage."

"We all come with baggage." He brushed his cheek against the back of her hand. "I have an ex-wife and a son, remember?"

"It's not the same. I'm sure you tried very hard to

make your marriage a success. Bunny told me—'' she blushed ''—that you didn't want the divorce, that you wanted to stay married and work things out. But Coreena was adamant—''

''And with no-fault divorce, I couldn't fight it,'' Gil finished for her. ''But don't blame Coreena for our divorce. Our marriage was a mistake from the start. We were so young and we married for the wrong reasons.'' He lowered her hand, but retained it, warming it with his.

''What reasons?''

''I married Coreena because she was very pretty and very sexy and my father hated her.'' His voice was grim. ''I was much too immature to marry.''

''How old were you?'' She stopped trying to pull away.

''Twenty.''

''That is young.'' Her low velvety voice worked on him as it always did.

''But I'm nearly thirty now.'' He gazed into her sober brown eyes. ''I know better now what I want. I want you, Patience. In the few short months we've known each other, you've brought so much…light— and I guess it's hope—into my life.''

''I haven't done anything—''

''You've helped Darby more than anyone else ever has. He's a much happier kid now.'' It lifted his spirits to finally state this truth out loud. ''It's all due to you. I know it is.''

She tried to interrupt.

"In all the years after our divorce," he forged on, "I've never gotten along with Coreena so well. I couldn't believe this year how calmly we discussed how to handle Darby's Christmas. It was like a miracle." His voice reflected his awe at this.

"Darby loves his mom and you very much." Patience looked away. "You two are lucky to have him."

He kissed her hand again and then drew it up, stroking his cheek with her palm. "That's what I mean. You saw my son as he is, a child in need of love and care. You didn't just dismiss him as a problem to be dealt with. You saw him as a lovable child. You accepted him, loved him."

The murmur and gurgle of voices from below and the wind gusting and prickling against the second-story windows made a soothing white noise.

Patience gazed with wonder as Gil bent and again kissed first one of her hands and then the other and pressed each side of his face in turn into her palms.

Her pulse shimmered through her and she felt herself softening to his tender touch. She bent over his bowed head. Pulling one hand free, she ran her fingers through the bittersweet chocolate of his hair and pressed a kiss into the curls tangled around her fingers.

"Gil," Patience whispered, "you are so tempting to me. I shouldn't care about you…but I do." She kissed his hair again. "I've avoided becoming attached... I've always kept my distance from anyone I might have...fallen in love with.

"Gil, I'm not a good bet." Her voice caught in her throat. "I won't marry unless I'm convinced that it's to someone like my uncle Mike—a loving man, a man of God. That's the only way it could work, because I know nothing of how to be a wife or mother. My own mother was a bad example, and Aunt Mary got sick and died before I was ready. I feel like I could have learned even more from her."

"Martina's past doesn't matter to me and I am capable of love, Patience. I love you. You're right, though. I haven't been close to God for a long time."

He paused. "People were so unkind when I married Coreena and so rejecting when she divorced me. It's hard to keep going to church when all you see are disapproving stares."

He pressed his lips to her hand again. "But I didn't feel the same this Sunday, and Darby was excited that I had come with him. I'd always sent him to Sunday school on the weekends he was with me. I didn't talk about God at home, but I didn't want him to grow up without God. My mother taught me that much."

He raised his head and kissed the inside of her wrist. "We deserve a chance, Patience. Both of us."

She trembled at his gentle touch.

"Your past and mine shouldn't mean we don't get

a future.'' He gazed into her eyes and then tried to kiss her mouth.

"Gil.'' She pulled back. "I don't want to make promises I can't keep. You don't know the true me. You don't know the deep well of unforgiveness that I hold against my mother. I don't have the emotional reserves to make love last a lifetime. And I won't settle for less.''

"You're fencing with me.'' Gil clung to her hands. "Have you forgotten why we are up here? Partly to get away from my dad. I'm having trouble forgiving my remaining parent, too. I don't know if I have the emotional maturity it takes to make love last, either. Don't you see, Patience? We won't know if we don't even try.''

"But—''

He silenced her with a kiss.

She sighed against his lips, unable to stop herself from kissing him. A thousand thoughts, sensations poured through her consciousness, but the only thing that seemed real were Gil's lips, so firm and insistent.

He gripped her shoulders fiercely and tenderly at the same time.

She rubbed her cheek against his, reveling in the chafing against his stubbly chin, this masculine texture.

"Gil,'' she breathed.

He placed kisses up her throat and then her sensitive earlobe and finally, dipped to touch her nape.

She sighed, clutching his shoulders.

He pulled her deeper into their embrace and buried his nose behind her ear. "Patience," he whispered, "we don't have to go fast. Why don't we just take it day by day? If this isn't going to work out, we'll know soon enough. I don't think divorce is an unforgivable sin and I don't think you should take the sins of your mother onto your life."

"Gil, I—"

"We'll take it slow." He pressed another kiss to her nape, breathing in her delicious fragrance. "And I'll come back to church and get myself straight with God again. Ever since He brought you into my life, I've felt the anger and hurt over my divorce draining away from me."

"Gil, I—" she repeated.

"Don't limit God, Patience. Christ died for my sins, past, present and future." Then he recited an old memory verse: "'If we confess our sins, God is faithful and just to forgive us and cleanse us from all unrighteousness.' First John 1:9. Don't limit God."

Tears leaked from her eyes and she bent her forehead to his. "Gil, Gil." She kissed his dark eyebrows.

Suddenly, a pounding of footsteps on the back stairs. Patience jerked away from Gil and stood up, wiping her tears away with her fingertips.

"Patience! Gil!" Bunny called from the kitchen. "Coreena just called. She's at the E.R. with Darby."

* * *

At Gil's side, Patience entered the brightly lit emergency entrance at the small local hospital. His ex-wife and her boyfriend were pacing the corridor. Coreena's eyes were swollen and red from crying. Blaine stood beside her, grim and protective.

Patience offered him her hand. "What happened?"

"Yes, what happened?" Gil echoed her.

Patience recognized the tight rein Gil was exerting over his tone of voice. Not a note of condemnation contaminated his concern for his son. *Thank you, Father. Don't let Darby be seriously hurt and don't let what had happened spoil the healing You've begun between Gil and Coreena.*

"Darby," Blaine said, a touch of defensiveness in his voice, "was outside playing in the snow."

"At this hour?" Gil objected.

"It's a holiday," Blaine growled. "The kid could stay up as long as he wanted."

"He was right in my small yard." Coreena sniffled into a crushed tissue. "I'd just told him he had another five minutes and then he had to come in for hot cocoa and bed."

"Anyway—" Blaine picked up the thread "—he climbed up the metal steps and for some reason decided to use the railing as a monkey bar. He hooked his knees on top and tried to do a complete circle around. He ended up hitting his forehead as he swung down."

"There was blood everywhere," Coreena moaned.

"I told her head wounds bleed a lot," Blaine continued, putting an arm around Coreena. "That some ice and an antiseptic would take care of it. But she wanted a doctor to look him over—"

"I didn't know how hard he hit his head." Coreena's voice shook. "He might have gotten a concussion—"

"No concussion," a doctor interrupted them, coming out of an examining area only a few feet away. "I didn't even put in any stitches. I just used some butterfly bandages. The edges of the wound were clean and were already pulling back together."

Patience sighed her relief.

"You mean it's not serious?" Coreena began weeping harder.

"No, just normal kid stuff." The young doctor grinned. "You can take him home. He'll be fine. He'll just have an interesting scar over one eyebrow. It'll give his face character."

"Thank you, Doctor," Coreena said, shaking his hand.

Gil echoed this, visibly relaxing at Patience's side.

The doctor hurried to a nurse who was motioning for him.

"Well, let's get our boy," Blaine said, waving his hand toward the examining area the doctor had come from.

Patience took Gil's hand and led him to Darby.

The little guy looked tired. A bandaged cut over one eyebrow was stark against his pale face. "Hi, Daddy."

Coreena took one of her son's hands and Darby reached for Patience's hand. "Hi, Miss Andrews. I got hurt."

"I know. But you're going to be fine, the doctor says." Patience smoothed back his hair.

Coreena mimicked the action on the other side of his head.

"Mommy, Miss Andrews is my friend," Darby said.

Coreena looked at Patience. "I know she is."

"Darn right she is," Blaine rumbled from behind.

Patience smiled over her shoulder at the big man.

Gil cleared his throat. "We're sorry you had to get hurt on Christmas Eve, son."

Darby nodded. "Mommy, can we go home now?"

Coreena looked at Gil. "I guess I shouldn't have bothered you, but I thought you'd want to know…"

"I appreciate it." Gil patted his son's back and then touched Coreena's shoulder. "You go home with your mom and get to sleep. Santa can't come unless you're in bed and snoring, you know."

Darby gave his dad a faint grin. "You're not mad at me?"

Gil moved forward and lifted his son into his arms for a quick hug. "Accidents happen, Darby. Just be more careful next time, okay? I think you scared your mom."

Patience silently rejoiced at Gil's every healing word.

"That's for sure," Coreena muttered.

Gil hugged his son once more and then turned and offered him to Blaine. The big man lifted Darby into his arms and gave Gil a gruff nod.

The five of them trailed out into the cold, windy night, and after exchanging "Merry Christmases" hurried through the wind to their vehicles. Gil drove away.

"Thanks for not being angry with Coreena." Patience sighed long and low. "She looked crushed."

Gil reached for Patience's hand and squeezed it. She leaned back against the seat and closed her eyes. It had been quite a Christmas Eve. Fatigue stole away her starch and she gave a languid sigh.

Shortly, Gil pulled up in front of Bunny's house and parked. He kept the engine running, with the heater holding the harsh cold at bay. Houses up and down the street glowed with colorful Christmas lights, bathing them in a holiday radiance.

She reached for the door handle, suddenly shy with this man. *Did I really let him kiss me?* "You don't need to walk me—"

"Wait. Patience, I have something for you." He pulled out a small jewelry box and handed it to her.

Her heart hammered, sending out the alarm she always experienced when a man got too close to her heart. *Don't offer me a ring. You said we'd take our time.* "Gil, I don't have anything for you," she objected, trying to make this act seem less momentous.

"Open it," he begged. "Please."

"But…" She tried to hand the box back to him, her hand trembling.

Raising a shoulder, he braced his hands on the steering wheel. "Open it."

She stared at his unrelenting profile and then at the tiny velvet box. Seconds ticked by on the green-glowing dashboard clock. At last, she untied the thin silver bow and opened the ring case. "Oh, Gil, it's lovely." *Not what I feared at all.*

"It's a vintage art deco ring, white-gold filigree and diamond chips. Try it on. We may have to have it sized."

"But Gil, this must have cost you a fortune." She tried to fight the elegant ring's attraction, but she was sunk. She wanted this ring, longed to wear it.

"I bought it at Caruthers's shop." Gil still faced forward. "And the cost doesn't matter. Put it on." Then he glanced at her.

Lord, is this what you want? Should I accept this gift? Feeling as in a dream, she started to slip the ring on her right hand.

"No, put it on your left ring finger." Gil slid closer to her. *Would she accept it, him?* "It's a promise ring."

"A promise ring?" She paused, holding the ring up in the dim light.

"Yes, when the time comes, when we've taken time to get to know each other and trust each other, I'll replace it with an engagement ring." When she didn't reply, he coaxed, "Please, Patience, just give us a chance."

She offered the ring back to him.

His heart fell.

"If it's a promise ring," she murmured, "then shouldn't *you* place it on my finger?"

Relief and joy surged through him, speeding his pulse. He took the ring and slid it onto the third finger of her left hand. "It's a perfect fit," he said, feeling how dry his mouth was.

She nodded.

He leaned toward her and silently asked permission.

She blushed and slanted forward, offering him her lips.

"Thank you, Patience," he whispered and kissed her. *Thank you, Lord, for second chances.*

Gil steeled himself to the task before him. It was 8:00 a.m. on Christmas morning. Within an hour, he'd be picking up Darby and bringing him home for Christmas. On their way, he would pick up Patience so she could watch his son open his presents. But before another day passed that held the possibility of Darby's being wounded, he needed to have it out once and for all with his father.

He knocked on the Captain's back door and waited in the winter chill.

His dad opened the door. "What do you want?" he barked.

"We need to talk." Gil pushed his way into the house.

"Have you come to apologize for the scene you created last night?" the Captain demanded.

"I could ask you the same question. No, I've come to tell you how it's going to be from now on." Gil pulled off his leather gloves.

"So you've assumed command here?" his father objected.

"I'm in command of my life and my son, so you need to know about a few changes I'm making."

"What changes?"

"Last night I asked Patience to allow me to—" Gil groped for the right word "—court her."

"Well, good," the Captain blustered. "About time—"

"I'm glad you approve—"

"Bunny thinks highly of Patience. She's worth a hundred of your first wife."

"That's enough. No more Coreena-bashing." Gil's hands became fists. "She is Darby's mother and if you keep this up, *you're* the one who's going to lose. No boy is going to let anyone speak against his mother. Didn't you hear him yelling, 'My mommy doesn't have bad blood'?"

A taut silence.

"Yes," the Captain finally admitted, scowling. "But it's the truth. Why you ever married that—"

"I wouldn't have married Coreena," Gil interrupted, "if you hadn't made her irresistible by telling me how bad she would be for me."

"So it's my fault you married her?" The Captain glared.

"No." Gil inhaled, pushing down his aggravation. "That was my decision and I'm the one, along with Darby, who has to live with it. But Patience has taught me to respect Coreena as Darby's *beloved mommy* and I'm not going to be foolish enough to alienate my son."

"I suppose you're going to say that's what I've done." His father stalked to the kitchen window and looked out the frosted glass.

A flow of heated words clogged Gil's throat. He swallowed them down. "The past is past. We only have each day. Do you want to alienate me? I don't want to alienate you."

"I have a right to my opinions." The Captain folded his arms. "You'll never make me say what I think is wrong is right."

"I'm not trying to tell you how to think or what to say. I'm only asking that you not say things you know will hurt Darby and turn him against you. And if you want a relationship with him, you'll heed my advice."

"If I can't say anything nice, don't say anything at

all,'' his father intoned with liberal sarcasm. "Is that
what this amounts to?''

"Yes.'' Gil pulled on his gloves again.

The Captain turned to face him.

They stared at each other. Gil didn't give an inch.

"Are you picking up Darby at that—'' the Captain
made a face "—at his mother's trailer?''

"Yes, and then I'm going to pick up Patience so
she can watch Darby open his presents. Do you want
to join us?''

"Yes, I would.''

Good. Just don't forget what I've said.

Through the icy night, Patience let Gil walk her to
Bunny's back door, home from the county club's New
Year's Eve gala. She unlocked it and led him upstairs
to her apartment. Her kitchen clock read 2:34 a.m.

"It was a lovely evening,'' she whispered even
though they were alone. Her hushed tone seemed ap-
propriate for this special occasion. She'd never gone
out with someone on a "real'' New Year's Eve date.

Gil gathered her into his arms. "It's late. I should
go.'' But he made no move to leave her. He pressed
his cheek next to hers.

She brushed against it, relishing the contact. She
drew in a delicious breath and then sighed with complete satisfaction. "I never knew I could feel like this.
I never let myself get this close to anyone....''

"I'm glad," his voice rumbled in her ear. "I want you all to myself. Selfish, I guess."

Lifting her mouth to him, she initiated a kiss, something she hadn't done before. It made her feel bold, powerful…

He prolonged the meeting of their lips. An arm around her waist, he pulled her even closer to him. Patience rested her head on his shoulder, feeling as she never had before. "You take my breath away."

"Ditto."

The phone rang.

They both froze. Phone calls at this hour couldn't be good. Had something happened to Darby sleeping over at the Captain's?

She reached for the kitchen wall phone and picked up. "Yes?"

Gil still held her other hand.

"Oh, Patience," Bunny said, "I'm sorry to bother you, but I heard you come in."

"What's wrong?"

"Your mother went out this evening and hasn't come back. Do you know where she is?"

Chapter Twelve

Patience was fading into numbness. Not only her body from the chill wintry night, but her spirit as well. Where was her mother? Would they find her before someone found out she was violating the parole terms that demanded she stay sober?

In the dark of the very early morning hours, Patience glanced at Gil who was driving her to yet another of the bars scattered around the unincorporated areas of the county. *Gil, why couldn't you have gone home before Bunny called? I don't want you here doing this with me.*

But how could she have managed without him and without a car? *And I'm a coward. I don't want to face my mother alone if she's been drinking.*

He turned to her. "Are you all right? You're awfully quiet." His face was ghostly in the moonlight that reflected off the snow.

"It's just...I hadn't done this for years." *Not since I was fifteen, when I finally ran away from her once and for all. Or that's what I had hoped I'd accomplished. How did I know then that I'd never be able to outrun my mother? Never be free.*

"It will be all right." Gil patted her arm.

No, it will never be all right. In the dim light, she tried to hide her despair with a little smile that pained her rigidly clenched jaw.

An hour or more ago—*What time was it anyway?*—they'd started their search at the small neighborhood bar on the far corner of the town square. It was the only one within walking distance of Bunny's.

The gray-bearded bartender there had recognized Martina and told them she'd left with a man he didn't know well. Martina had ridden off in the man's truck—a disturbing development. So Gil had offered to drive Patience around to see if they could find Martina and bring her home, safe.

Patience tried to beat down the fear that jammed up her throat. *It shouldn't worry me. She's done this as long as I can recall. What's new?*

Gil pulled up into one of the few vacant spots in another bar's parking lot. Bars out in the county didn't have to close at 2:00 a.m. like the ones in town, so the sound of music seeped out from inside the old farmhouse that now served as a bar. He got out and she joined him in walking to the garishly neon-lit entrance. When Gil opened the door, a country-western song, "Stand by Your Man," cannonaded over them.

Childhood memories of roaming from bar to bar in their run-down Chicago neighborhood looking for her mother surged through Patience. Humiliation clutched her heart. *I don't want to do this again. I never wanted to do this again. Never.*

Inside the crowded tavern, she approached the bartender, a beefy man with a ponytail. In the rip-roaring New Year's Eve din, she shouted, "I'm looking for my mother." She offered him a photo Bunny had taken of them at Christmas.

He glanced at the picture and then handed it back. "No idea," he yelled.

She scanned the darkened raucous room, hoping to glimpse her mother. But no, Martina wasn't here. She nodded her thanks to the man behind the bar and then she led Gil outside again. Shivering in the frigid pre-dawn, she inhaled the cold clean air after the smoky bar. She preceded Gil back to his car. "We might as well go home," she muttered.

"But going off with a stranger…" Gil helped her into the passenger side. "Your mother might be in danger."

"This is just her same old pattern. Go out, start drinking and hook up with any willing male." Patience didn't try to keep the scorn, hopelessness out of her voice. "It's something no sane woman would do in this day and age of serial murderers and rapists.

But my mother is fearless when she's had a few." Patience shut the door against the January cold. Bitterness burned her throat raw.

Gil climbed behind the wheel. "Let's try one more, and then if we don't find her I'll just call the sheriff and ask him to keep an eye out for her—"

"No!" Patience's heart pounded. "Her drinking again violates her terms of parole! Even if *she* doesn't care, I don't want her to have to go back to prison."

He covered her hand with his. "All right. I won't contact him." He started the engine and flipped the heater on high.

"Gil, I don't want you to do anything you shouldn't as an officer of the court." *Lord, how am I supposed to react? I know You want me to forgive her. But how can I when she's started drinking again? How can I forgive someone who doesn't even care anything about herself? Or how she affects anyone else?*

"There are a few taverns out on the southbound highway." He backed out. "I'll head there."

"No." A tremendous feeling of heaviness finally overwhelmed Patience. "Just take me home. She'll show up eventually. She always does." Patience pressed her fist to her mouth so he wouldn't note her lips trembling. "Bad pennies always do."

"Patience, I don't mind driving around to a few more—"

"No, take me home. This is fruitless."

Gil turned the car around and headed back toward town. Patience bit into her fist to keep from venting her despair with spiteful yet hopeless words. The dark miles passed and the predawn gray lightened the horizon.

Patience felt a million years old, nearly dead.

When they drove through the town square on their way to Bunny's, the sight before her froze her heart. Ahead near the courthouse, swirling blue-and-white lights illuminated the early morning. Two officers, one she recognized as the sheriff, were dragging her mother up the steps to the county-jail door. Obviously intoxicated, Martina was staggering even though the officers on each side supported her under her arms.

Gil slowed the car and parked behind the patrol car. He looked to Patience.

She couldn't speak.

"I guess we better go in," Gil said.

She nodded.

He held her arm as he helped her out of the car and up the stone steps.

Tears wet her cheeks as she entered the jail.

"Don't...call my...daughter!" Ahead of them, Martina shouted in a slurred voice. "Miss Goody Two-shoes...out on the town with the...D.A. She won't want to...bail me out! What...did I do anyway, huh?"

"We're going to book you for driving without a license and under the influence of alcohol." Sheriff

Longworthy adjusted his arm under Martina's as she staggered.

"I had to drive," Martina said in a slurred voice. "That…jerk got the wrong idea. I just wanted a drinking buddy… A woman's got a right…to defend herself!"

Closing her eyes, Patience wanted to evaporate, disappear.

The two law officers succeeded in getting Martina through an inner doorway behind the counter, probably to be booked.

"So she not only violated her parole by drinking," Patience murmured to Gil, "but she also drove without a license and probably stole the vehicle." Wishing she could drop through the floor, Patience slid down to sit on a chair along the wall.

The deputy at the counter glanced over, obviously curious.

Gil sank down beside her. "I hate to see you suffer like this."

That's why you need to forget me and move on to someone else. This isn't ever going to change, is it, Lord? I belong to You, so I can't ever just turn my back on her, disown her. My mother's alcoholism is a life sentence for her—and for me.

Much later on New Year's Day after supper, Patience walked through the early darkness to see her mother in the county jail. Because of the holiday, she hadn't been able to bail out her mother. Though it wasn't a visiting day, the sheriff let her in at Gil's request.

Her mother watched the sheriff unlock her cell and let her daughter in.

Patience perched on the bare mattress across from her mother. "Are you able to talk?"

Martina turned her face away and didn't reply.

Patience stared around. The other cells were full and the other inmates were listening avidly, bored and hoping for an interesting scene between mother and daughter, a live soap opera for their enjoyment.

That was one of the worst things about being caught up in the judicial system. One lost all privacy. And dignity. Soon, in a court of law, in front of God and everybody, a lawyer would ask the sheriff to testify to the fact that Martina had violated the terms of her parole.

Fortunately for her mother, the man who'd picked her up and whom Martina had shoved out of his own truck hadn't wanted any more trouble. Once he got his truck back, he'd refused to press theft charges. So her mother wasn't facing any new charges.

Patience closed her eyes, trying to blot out the dismal surroundings and the avid audience. "Why did you do it, Mother?"

No reply.

"Why? Do you hate yourself that much?" *Hate* me *that much?*

"I can't be like you," her mother mumbled. "I can't stay straight. I've tried and it doesn't work. Just leave me alone. I don't have what it takes to be a mother. Never did. You know that best of all. Go on. Leave."

So they'd entered the guilt phase of the downward spiral. Patience could write the script herself, word by word, stage by stage. She braced herself. "I'm not staying long. I just wanted to see you myself. Is there anything you need?"

"No."

Patience pushed herself onto her feet. "Would you like me to pray with you?"

"No."

Then I'll pray for myself. God, I don't know how or why this has happened. But I know You can carry me through the shame and hopelessness. You're going to have to because I have no power of my own remaining to deal with this. It's beyond me.

A week and a half after the Christmas break, feathery snowflakes fluttered down outside the window of Patience's schoolroom where the squirrel had chattered all those months ago in the early fall. Her class was again busy copying down the week's spelling words.

Restless, Patience rose and walked up and down the aisles, observing her students. They'd grown up so much in the past few months. She paused by

Darby's desk, longing to stroke his dark waves, so much like his father's. Bent over his paper, Darby was concentrating on his work, no longer tempted by anything, not even the long braids of the girl sitting in front of him. *I care about you, Darby, but I can't let it show.*

He looked up and grinned at her.

With a nod, she resumed her walk around the room. Her mother was still in jail, awaiting a court date to appear before a judge to appeal the revocation of her parole. If the appeal didn't work, Martina would be returned to prison to begin serving the remainder of her sentence.

Patience tried to make this seem real, but it felt like a movie she was being forced to watch. Or like a nightmare she was having and screaming in her mind, "Wake up! Wake up!" But this wasn't a dream. It was her life, had always been and would always be.

At the end of the school day, Darby dawdled around his desk. Patience tried to ignore him and made much of concentrating on correcting the day's math assignment. *Go home, Darby. Please don't stop and talk to me again.*

"Teacher," Darby asked in a small voice. "Why don't you ever come over to my house anymore?"

"I've been very busy." She kept her gaze on the paper before her.

"I miss you, and Blaine wants to know what's wrong, too. Are we still friends?"

You're not going to make this easy, are you? Patience choked, suppressing the sudden urge to give in to tears.

"Darby, I'm still your friend." She said the words in a calm tone, completely at odds with her speeding pulse. "I've just been busy. Please say hi to your mom and Blaine." She glanced down at her naked ring finger. The promise ring Gil had given her was in a drawer in her bedroom. *I have to return it to him, but that would open them both up to explanation, recrimination…*

"I'm sure," Patience continued, "we'll see each other away from school sometime soon."

"Really?" Darby's face lit with hope. "How about this weekend?"

She shook her head.

Darby's chin fell.

Lord, I know I'm hurting him, but I don't have a choice. I care too much about him to inflict my problems on him…on Gil.

In the mid-January evening gloom, Gil waited at Bunny's front door, prepared to do battle—if he could only get Patience alone. He leaned on the bell.

Bunny finally answered his ring. Her naturally cheerful face looked grimmer than he'd ever seen it. Then she recognized him and her face brightened. "Thank God you've come."

"I'm here to see Patience—"

"Wonderful." Bunny pulled him inside with a hand on his arm. "I've been living in a funeral parlor since New Year's Eve. You're the only one who can do anything to get Patience out of the blue funk she's in. So do it. *Please.*"

I'm glad you have confidence in me. I don't. God, help me out here. I'm no good at talking outside a courtroom.

Bunny ushered him down the hall and through her kitchen to the back hall and then gave him a push toward the stairs. "Don't take no for an answer," Bunny whispered loudly. "And kiss her until she's silly—that's my advice."

With a nod of agreement, Gil mounted the steps, and with each one his determination to make things right with Patience strengthened. *I love her and I'm not letting her get away. And that's final.*

Just as he was about to knock on the door at the top of the stairs, he caught himself. Instead, he reached for the knob and walked in. She wouldn't be in the shower at this early hour, would she?

"Patience? It's me, Gil." In the open doorway, he waited on the threshold of the empty kitchen, a snappish chill flowing around his ankles.

"Gil?" She appeared in the opposite doorway in jeans and an oversize red sweater.

He stepped inside and shut the door behind him. His glasses fogged up and he swiped them with his sleeve.

''What are you doing here?'' Patience took a step toward him. ''Is something wrong? Another robbery? Darby?''

''Yes, something's wrong.'' He jerked off his coat and gloves and strode to her. ''You've been avoiding me since New Year's.'' He closed his hands around her arms just above the wrists. ''And it's got to stop. Now.''

Patience felt her resistance to this man, a stiffness, a resolve that she'd labored to build up over the past couple of weeks quake under his advance. *No. I can't give in.*

She wrested her arms from his grip. ''Gil—'' she made her voice steady and detached ''—unless you have something about the Putnam case, or some concern about Darby as my student, we have nothing to discuss.'' She faced him, not letting him come farther into her apartment.

''We're going to talk and that's final.'' Gil claimed her hands. ''And it has little to do with Putnam, but a lot to do with Darby, but not as your student, as your friend. I can't believe you've pushed us away. And over what? Do you think I care that your mother is an alcoholic? Or that I'll reject you because she may go back to prison?''

She tried to pull her cold hands from his chilled ones.

He hung on.

He wasn't playing fair. Didn't he know that there

were boundaries to be observed? Well, if he wanted to strip off the gloves, she could, too. "Gil, you once told me that you came with baggage, didn't you?"

He nodded.

"What if I've decided I don't want to...contend with your baggage? I don't need a man with an ex-wife and a son." She jerked away and went to the sofa.

She waited for his response, despising herself for the hateful words she'd just said. *I can't let him win this. Darby and he are better off without me and my mother and all her problems. I can't let him go all noble on me. He's like that. He married Coreena, ignoring the fact that she came with sad strings attached.*

He reached her again and sat down right beside her.

She moved out of his reach, pressing her back into the sofa arm opposite him. "No. Don't you get it? Our brief time together is over. I've thought all this through and it just won't work. I'll finish my year here and go back to Chicago and start fresh.

"I should have known," she continued, "that this wasn't going to work out right after the trial." *Or to be more exact, right after my mother appeared on Bunny's doorstep.* "My trouble is I just don't know when to quit—"

"I'm not letting you get away—" he interrupted.

"But I'm going to learn how to walk away, starting

now.'' She wrapped her arms around herself tightly. ''You should go home.''

''I'm not leaving until I've had my say.'' Gil reached to touch her cheek.

She turned her face away from his hand. ''Okay, have your say. And then leave.'' She made herself flood the final word with an iciness that sliced both ways—through him and through her own heart. *If I give an inch...*

''I know you're upset over your mother's...relapse and her legal problems.'' His tone implored her. ''I can understand that. But why do you think they have anything to do with us? I thought we'd worked this out. You are Patience. You are not your mother. I've fallen in love with you.''

His impassioned words burned like acid onto her spirit. *No, you can't love me. Let me go. I'll only bring you pain.*

She shook her head with vehemence. ''I'm sorry for you. But I can't love you.''

''Yes, you can and do. Why are you being so stubborn?'' He tried to enfold her.

She didn't let him. She kept her arms around herself, a barrier she wouldn't let him breach.

He possessed her anyway, his arms resting on her back, his chin on top of her head. He wouldn't release her. ''I'm not giving up. With you, my life makes sense. With you, Darby is happy. I'm not letting go.''

''You're wasting your time—''

He tried to kiss her.

She wrenched herself free.

He came after her.

Her heart racing, she held out her hands to fend him off. "I have a ring to return to you."

"I don't want your promise ring back." He started toward her again.

"No. I say no. Now leave." She gasped for breath. "Leave."

He was breathing hard also. He stared at her.

She looked back at him, but kept her hands out in front of herself.

"Very well. I'll leave...tonight. But I'll be back." He turned and hurried away, grabbing up his coat off the kitchen chair.

"If you keep this up," Patience shouted to his back, "I'll resign early. I won't be pushed."

At her door, he turned to glare at her. "I can be as stubborn as you." And then he slammed out of her apartment.

She sank to her knees, shaking. A sob tore through her, ripping at her heart, lungs, throat. *Why did You let me love him, Lord, just to lose him? Why did You let me glimpse heaven just to let my mother snatch it away?*

With the TV remote control in hand, Gil sat in his living room alone. He'd just put Darby down for the night. He clicked on the television and then from channel to channel. The canned laughter burst out in little spurts from show to show. He clicked the power button and he was in silence again.

He imagined Patience there with him, curled up beside him wearing those jeans and that oversize sweater she'd worn last night when he'd gone to her apartment. "Lord," he prayed aloud, "how do I get through to her? I can't let her go. Help me. I know I've not paid much attention to You over the past few years. But I know You have paid close attention to me. Help me. Show me the way. I need Patience in my life. I love her. Let me convince her."

The cell phone in his pocket trilled its tones.

He pulled it out and opened it. "Gil here."

"I'm on my way to 114 Oak Street," the sheriff growled. "A neighbor thinks there may be a robbery in progress."

Gil shot to his feet. "I'll be right there."

Chapter Thirteen

Riding a crest of adrenaline, Gil blew through stop signs and sped all the way to 114 Oak. Dan Putnam was free this time. Had he attacked again?

In front of the address, Gil parked helter-skelter in the midst of three abandoned sheriff cars. Their rotating blue-and-white lights bathed the darkened neighborhood in a ghostly light. People stood at windows peering out around curtains and shades.

Gil bounded out of his car, slipping and sliding on the ice and snow up to the house. He charged inside.

"Halt!" a familiar voice rang out from the shadowy rear of the entry hall.

"It's me, Sheriff. Gil Montgomery." Gil's pulse pounded in his ears. He gasped for breath, not just from running. Would this be it, could it be the last robbery?

"Come on back here," the sheriff said with glee in his voice. "We caught him red-handed."

Gil loped the few feet and stopped inside the brightly lit kitchen. He scanned the room crowded with blue uniforms. He saw an older gentleman on a kitchen chair with a large German shepherd sitting on the floor beside him. Then he saw a hunched-up Wade Bevin leaning against the sink in handcuffs. "Bevin?" Gil gawked at the man. *My witness for the prosecution? No.*

"Yeah, his luck ran out." The sheriff's voice pulsed with satisfaction. "Mr. Connolly has a very good watchdog. As Bevin broke into the kitchen, the dog attacked. He's a retired police dog and knew just how to subdue and hold a prisoner." The sheriff beamed at the German shepherd.

Mr. Connolly stroked the dog's tawny and brown-black head and murmured encouragement to him. "Nobody knew that about my pal here," the older man said with obvious pride.

"But he still knows his stuff. Don't you, boy? After he'd nabbed this creep—" Mr. Connolly motioned toward Bevin "—I called 911 and here we are. This scum won't be attacking and robbing any more of my neighbors. He ought to get a stiff sentence for what he did to Bertha Perkins." The man then voiced an uncomplimentary assessment of Bevin's character.

Gil silently echoed this. "How did Bevin get rid of the loot? Have you asked him yet?"

"Yes, and he's ready and willing to make a deal and implicate his accomplice." The sheriff smirked.

"Accomplice?" Gil stared at Bevin, fighting an undignified grin. *Better and better.* "Then let's take our suspect down to the station and get his statement on tape."

Later, still in the dark early-morning hours, Gil and the sheriff knocked on the door of the tidy Victorian home on Main Street and waited.

In the cold wind, Gil shifted, restless and eager.

The sheriff gave him an encouraging look and lift of his chin. "No problem," he mouthed. And then, "Don't sweat it."

As they waited, an upstairs and then a hall light glimmered to life. The door opened as wide as its restraining chain lock would permit.

The sheriff stabbed a document through the gap. "I'm serving you with a search warrant," he said with gruff authority. "Open up, Caruthers."

A shocked silence. The hand that had caught the papers clenched around them.

"Thank goodness," Caruthers breathed finally. "Come in."

Both the sheriff and Gil glanced at each other, the sheriff obviously as startled by Caruthers's response as Gil.

The door clicked shut and then reopened with the chain unhooked. "Did he try to rob a third person?"

"Who do you mean?" the sheriff barked as he and Gil entered.

"Bevin, of course." Caruthers fell back, giving them room. "The idiot."

"Are you saying that Wade Bevin committed more than the robbery tonight? That he was responsible for the first two also?" Gil pressed him.

"He robbed Mrs. Perkins and Mrs. Carmichael," Caruthers admitted without any show of emotion. "Who did he hit tonight?"

"If you knew—" Gil ignored the man's question "—that Wade Bevin was guilty of the Perkins robbery, why did you testify *against* Dan Putnam?" Anger knotted Gil's midsection.

"I didn't testify *against* Putnam." Caruthers's forehead puckered. "I merely testified that I'd done an appraisal for Mrs. Perkins and what I had found. I never said a word against Dan."

Gil absorbed Caruthers's convoluted reasoning. And shook his head. People always devised a way to justify their own actions. "You withheld evidence in a felony. That in itself is a felony, Caruthers."

"We're going to search your home and shop for evidence," the sheriff growled and moved closer to Caruthers.

"Oh, I'll show you where it is. No need to tear everything apart, looking." Caruthers's lifeless tone was unnerving.

The sheriff held up a hand, stemming Caruthers's

wordy flow and then recited the Miranda. "Now don't try to say I didn't warn you. The D.A. is my witness."

"You act like you've been expecting this." Gil looked at the antique dealer, dressed in a luxurious robe and slippers. He didn't appear capable of committing any crime. But then Gil noticed the man's hand shook as it held the warrant. And he had dark circles under his eyes.

Caruthers considered Gil for a moment and then drew a shuddering breath. "Montgomery, this experience has been like getting on a horse and finding out it's an unbroken mustang. I initiated this…train of regrettable events. I appraised Mrs. Perkins's antiques and wanted to possess them. But *not* pay for them. Greed, simple greed has been my downfall."

Gil remained silent, letting Caruthers indict himself. He'd been warned.

The man closed his eyes as though recruiting his nerve. "Bevin had done some handyman work for me and I got the impression that he might be amenable to…easy cash. And he lived at Mrs. Perkins's house. He had access. And everyone knew that Bertha and her son had been arguing."

Caruthers stopped the abundant flow of incriminating words and sucked in air. "Bevin robbed and attacked Mrs. Perkins. I didn't want that to happen! Why didn't he just wait until she was in bed? Why hit an old woman over the head? Cause her to have a stroke? Senseless."

"You tell us," the sheriff suggested.

"Because he has a nasty mean streak." The dealer shut his mouth. "I didn't notice that until I was already in too deep to get out."

The man sank down on the carpeted steps behind him and lowered his head into his hands. "But it's been out of my control since then. And I've been living in fear ever since Bevin attacked Mrs. Carmichael."

"Why?" Gil asked, though he thought he knew the answer already.

"Because I was the only one who could testify against him." Caruthers sounded in pain, fear. "He's been demanding money from me. When I couldn't give it to him, he decided to commit more robberies."

"Why did he demand money from you?" the sheriff asked. "Blackmail?"

"No, not really blackmail." Caruthers glanced up. "It's just because I hadn't dealt with a fence before. I wasn't able to get rid of most of the stolen items quickly. I couldn't give him what I'd promised—not immediately! I had to be discreet and careful." Caruthers made a face.

"Bevin," the antique dealer continued, "has little understanding of my difficulties and was impatient to receive his share of what I would realize when I finally sold the stolen items. So when I didn't pay him, he began demanding I advance him money or he said he'd commit more robberies and implicate me if he was caught." Caruthers rubbed his forehead and stared at the oak floor. "Gentlemen, it's been a nightmare."

The man sounded sincere. Gil and the sheriff exchanged glances.

"So where's the stuff?" the sheriff prompted.

"Follow me." With slumping shoulders, Caruthers led them through his kitchen and down the steep rickety steps into his old brick basement. "There's a false wall here where I hide valuable pieces."

Then just like in a movie, he pushed a bit of molding, and a panel swung open. "I don't know why the original owners had this put in. I've wondered a few times if this is an old stop on the Underground Railroad or just a place they liked to hide valuables also."

On shelves in the cubbyhole were many antiques and jewelry boxes. The sheriff scanned the shelves and turned to Caruthers. "We'll still be searching your shop and this house. We can't just take your word that this is all you are concealing."

Caruthers opened his lips to object but then paused, wide-mouthed. "I guess," he said finally, "I have no choice but to accept this. You can't dance with the devil and come away squeaky clean." The man suddenly looked drawn and older. "Do you think…will this mean jail time?"

"That's not for us to say. Bevin is trying to get a deal from us for implicating you." Gil tried not to feel any sympathy for Caruthers. His greed had caused such grief for so many, mainly Mrs. Perkins and her son, Dan. Also for Patience, the woman he loved. "So far we're not making any deals with anyone."

A few hours later, early Sunday morning, Gil gripped Patience's arm as he led her into the inner room at the courthouse. He hoped she'd react the way he wanted her to. Being so close and feeling her resistance pained him, like bumping repeatedly into an ice wall.

"Why won't you tell me why you've brought me here?" Patience, dressed in jeans and a black sweater, sounded upset, resentful. "Does this have anything to do with my mother's case?"

Lord, let this day spark a change for the better in Patience. She's been hurt badly and I love her so. "No, I told you this has something to do with the Putnam case."

"What? What does it have to do with Dan Putnam?" Patience glared at him as if he were persecuting her.

He refused to answer, but pulled her along until they reached the evidence room. He tried to hide his reaction to her scent, her voice, everything about her that beckoned to him.

He pulled out a key from his pocket, unlocked the steel dead-bolt-locked door and ushered her inside. "Look at this shelf." He pointed to a shelf, undusty in the dusty room because it had just been put to use. Tagged vases, art glass, porcelain and jewelry dotted the shelf.

She gazed up at the items. Her lips parted.

He let her go and she inched toward the shelf as though not believing what she was seeing.

"Don't touch anything," he cautioned as he watched her. The black of her sweater made her look paler than usual in the stark fluorescent lighting.

"What am I looking at?" She turned her wondering eyes to him. "Did someone find more stolen antiques?"

He grinned, suddenly unable to suppress his mounting joy. "We caught a suspect right in the act of a third robbery." He heard her quick intake of breath.

"Who?"

"Wade Bevin." Saying the name irked him. Bevin had lied to him and Gil wasn't about to forget it.

"You mean—" Patience looked thoughtful "—one of Mrs. Perkins's roomers?"

He nodded again, his throat tight. *Patience, I need you, want you.*

"Where did he keep this stuff?" she asked, facing Gil. "He couldn't have kept it in his room at Mrs. Perkins's house." She looked suddenly vulnerable.

He held himself back from going to her. "He didn't. His accomplice did."

Patience's mouth formed an O. "Who?"

"Vincent Caruthers."

Patience gasped and covered her mouth with her hands.

Then Gil went on to explain all that had brought them to this room and all each lawbreaker had had to say about each other.

"So Vincent Caruthers's greed started all this misery?" she asked.

"Yes, when he saw the things Mrs. Perkins had, he wanted them and he didn't want to pay her for them." Gil propped his hands on his hips, again holding himself back from Patience. The pain he'd seen in her eyes earlier when he'd picked her up had cut him through the heart. "But I'm afraid he's already paid a steep price for his greed."

"How?" Uncertainty trembled in her low voice.

"It's cost him his peace of mind." Gil took one step closer to her. "He was in fear of Bevin and now he may face jail time. At the very least, his reputation as an honest appraiser and dealer is ruined. He'll never be trusted again."

Patience looked down and shoved her hands in the back pockets of her jeans. "Have you told Dan Putnam yet?"

"No, I wanted you to go with me to give him the good news." He gazed at her. "Will you?" *Come with me, Patience. You deserve to be a part of my giving him his good news. You started all this.*

She stared at Gil.

"You're the one who believed in Dan." Gil injected an extra shot of firmness into his voice. "You're the one who kept him from being convicted on a false charge. You should be there with me when I tell him."

She kept her hands in her pockets and stared at the dull gray linoleum. "Okay." Her restrained tone told him nothing of her feelings.

The drive to Dan Putnam's modest house took only a few minutes. Patience sat in silence, hugging the opposite door from him. Gil prayed as he drove, *Lord, please use this to speak to this woman I love and who has suffered so much pain and sorrow over this case and her mother.*

Looking first surprised and then worried at seeing them, Dan let them in to his bungalow. He motioned them toward a sagging couch in the small, cluttered living room. He perched on a straight-back chair. "So what can I do for you?"

"We're here to do something for you," Gil said after clearing his voice.

"Oh?" Dan sounded suspicious.

I don't blame you. Again, Gil regretted prosecuting this innocent man. *Patience was right. I banked on his history of mental illness. I know better now.*

Patience nodded encouragement.

Gil took a deep breath. "We arrested Wade Bevin last night—"

"Wade?" Dan's face screwed up in shock, disbelief. "For what?"

"He was apprehended in the act of committing a third robbery last night."

Patience smiled at Dan.

"A third? You mean, Wade…" Dan said in a flustered "I can't believe this" tone. "Who was last night's victim?"

"Mr. Connelly on Oak," Patience replied before Gil. "Do you know him?"

Dan nodded. "Is he all right?" he asked in a concerned voice.

"Fine," Gil said. "His German shepherd is a retired police dog and knew just how to handle an intruder. Bevin didn't know that."

Dan stood up abruptly and took a turn around the small, muddled room. "Does that mean…"

"First thing on Monday morning," Gil informed him, "I'll start the ball rolling to have you appear before the judge and be acquitted as soon as possible."

"I…I," Dan stuttered, "I can't thank you enough."

"Thank this lady." Gil beamed at Patience. "She's the one who believed you."

"I do." Dan sought her hand and wrung it. "Thank you, Miss Andrews. I know this hasn't been easy for you."

"No need to thank me." Patience blushed, looking pleased. "I was just fulfilling my duty as a juror."

"You did more than that." Dan still held her hand.

Patience, still blushing, tried to retrieve her hand.

But Dan wouldn't let go. He appeared unconscious of the way he was gripping her.

Patience stopped fighting Dan and let him keep her hand. Silence.

Gil waited to see what would happen next.

"What will you do now, Mr. Putnam?" Patience asked finally.

"I have my mother to take care of." Dan released her finally and sat down on the same chair. "She is making some progress." His tone faltered.

"This should help heal the breach," Gil suggested.

Dan shook his head. "My mother already knew I didn't attack her."

Gil could have kicked himself. Of course she did. Just because she couldn't tell the sheriff that didn't mean she didn't know the truth of who had attacked her.

"But we still have a history of hurting each other." Dan propped his elbows on his knees and cradled his chin in his hands.

"You're going to stay in Rushton?" Patience asked gently.

"Yes, I can't make things right from miles away." Dan sighed with weariness. "You've both heard all about my history of mental illness and how my mother has always been…ashamed and embarrassed by it."

Patience nodded.

Gil thought of his own father and their history. Then he recalled the pain he'd seen on Patience's face, heard in her voice the night they'd searched bars for Martina. Why did parents and children rub against each other so?

"I still hope that someday we will be able to have a…better relationship," Dan ventured. "Maybe not great, but at least not hurtful to each other."

Gil hoped the same for Patience and her mother. *How can I convince Patience she has a right to a life of her own, Lord?*

"We were trying," Dan continued, "and then I got upset about my bankruptcy. I should have had more faith."

"That happens to all of us at times," Patience murmured.

Gil thought Dan's words applied to each of them. He'd started having more faith in God and in his ex-wife and Darby's life had improved. *God, help me have more trust in you.*

"My mother needs me now more than ever," Dan said simply.

"How about your bankruptcy?" Gil asked, unable to stifle his curiosity about the man's plans.

"I'll go ahead and finish filing for it." Dan rubbed his chin. "I don't have much choice. I'll find some way to make a living. God will provide."

"He always has for me." Patience's voice lifted with a firmness, an evident faith.

Gil listened in silence. *Lord, you've provided Patience for me. Help me persuade her that we have a future together.*

Dan nodded. "Leaving Rushton now would be vindictive and self-destructive." He half smiled. "A few years of counseling haven't been wasted on me. Living with an unforgiving attitude would only damage both my mother and me even more."

"You're a better person than I am," Patience admitted, combing her bangs with her fingers in a nervous gesture.

"It's always hardest to forgive those who have hurt us most." Dan sat up straighter. "But unforgiveness is not a healthy way to live."

Impressed, Gil rose and offered Dan his hand. "No hard feelings?"

"None." Dan stood and shook Gil's hand.

Gil took Patience's elbow and moved them through the door into the cold clear morning. "Well, where do we go from here, Patience?"

Chapter Fourteen

In the chill morning, Gil accepted the hand Patience offered him and walked her to his car. Then he drove them away, not really having a destination in mind. But at least he knew what he wanted—Patience back with him. Sitting near him, she still held his hand in hers and that meant more to him than anything else at this moment. *Lord, give me the right words. Help me convince her we have a right to love each other.*

Finally, he pulled into an empty parking lot off the deserted square. A few people were parking on the street in front of the church. The square would soon be filled with early service churchgoers.

Dan Putnam's words about forgiving played over in Gil's mind. "I feel so awful over prosecuting an innocent man. And such a good man. Putnam makes me feel guilty for the anger I hold against my own father."

"Same here," Patience whispered.

Gil reached for her and pulled her into a relaxed embrace. He didn't feel he needed to clutch her to him. He didn't think she'd be pulling away. Not after Dan had softened them with his words about love and forgiveness.

But had Dan's words hit Patience the same way? Or must he still persuade her?

Gil smoothed back her short silken hair. "Patience, we have something precious between us, something from God. I have a sincere love for you. I know that because my son and I have mourned deeply the loss of you in our lives. Please come back to us."

"I'm sorry. I never meant to hurt anyone." She rested her cheek on his chest and gazed upward.

"I know you didn't." He pressed a kiss to her forehead. "But our love is worth fighting for. I'm not letting you shut me out again. Ever."

"I didn't stop loving you, Gil." She sighed and snuggled closer to him in the wintry chill. "I just...I just didn't want you to have to deal with my mother.... I didn't want to drag you through the mess she's created—"

"We're going to be family." Gil framed her face between his two hands. "I said before that we'd take our time and work out this loving each other. I'm not the same man who married Coreena for all the wrong reasons." He kissed her forehead.

"We'll take our time," he promised, "go to counseling, work things out. Then when it comes time to make our promises to each other, we'll be ready to keep our love strong for a lifetime.''

''But I don't know—'' she tried to look away, but he wouldn't let her ''—what's going to happen to my mother. She could easily go back to prison.''

''As long as you and I are free to love each other, that doesn't matter. Patience, there will never be a perfect time for us to give our hearts to one another. Because life isn't ever going to be perfect.'' He kissed her lips.

She clung to him. ''I wanted it to be perfect for you.'' Tears filled her golden-brown lashes.

''Same here. But we're only human.'' He kissed her forehead, her cheek, her lips. ''We can only control us, our feelings and our actions. We can't control other people or circumstances.''

''You're right.'' Patience pulled the promise ring he'd given her for Christmas out of her jean pocket and offered it to him. Then she placed it in his hand.

With a rush of joy, Gil slid the ring onto her slender finger. ''Patience, I love you no matter what.''

''Gil, I love you no matter what.''

Epilogue

Gracie's spring wedding day had come. Patience stood at the front of the familiar sactuary between the other bridal attendants. To Patience's right, Annie, Gracie's sister, the matron of honor, was closest to the bride. To Patience's left was Connie, Gracie's best friend. As usual, Patience felt like a blond Amazon among her dark-haired, petite cousins and Connie who was a pretty brunette. Gracie's dress was elegant white satin without any fussy frills. Patience, Connie and Annie wore pale mint green dresses, also in satin.

The fragrance of lilies wafted through the church. Tomorrow would be Easter and the church was adorned for that holy celebration. The pastor was leading Gracie and Jack through their vows—"...for better for worse..."

Patience blinked back tears. The familiar church in

Uncle Mike's neighborhood was crowded with friends and relatives. Gil and Darby had driven north with her for the wedding. She was staying at Uncle Mike's, and the groom's mother had taken in Gil and Darby.

Unfortunately, Martina's prediction that she wouldn't be attending Gracie's wedding had come true. Martina was back in prison, serving her sentence. Patience had visited her the week after she'd been returned to prison and they were writing to each other. *Lord, you'll have to take charge of my mother. I still hope she'll turn her life over to you. But that has to be her decision. I can't make it for her.*

Patience listened to Gracie repeating her vows, and then Connie moved to a pulpit to one side and read the love passage from First Corinthians, Chapter Thirteen, "'Love is patient. Love is kind...'" Connie's sweet voice gave each phrase special meaning.

Patience was now secure in Gil and Darby's love. And Gracie was marrying the man she'd loved for years. Patience said a prayer that Connie would also find a man who would appreciate her. *That's up to you, of course, Father. But Connie deserves someone special.*

After closing the Bible, Connie walked back to her place beside Patience. The pastor began blessing the new couple. Patience prayed along with him, wishing her cousin and her husband a long, joy-filled life together.

"Amen. I now wish to present to you Mr. and Mrs.

Jack Lassater,'' the minister announced proudly. The wedding party turned to face the congregation. The organ boomed out the postlude and after Annie had arranged the bridal train, Gracie and Jack started down the steps.

Patience brushed away a happy tear. Life had finally come together for her—in God's timing. Her life might not be perfect, but soon she would be gaining a husband and a son. She would reap what she always longed for—a family of her very own.

On the bride's side of the church, Darby stood up and waved to Patience. She waved back. Gil beamed at her and her heart fluttered with excitement and happiness. *Thank you, Father. I'm sorry I doubted Your power to turn our ashes into joy.*

* * * * *

Look for the last story in the
SISTERS OF THE HEART
series by Lyn Cote,
LOVING CONSTANCE,
coming in November 2004.

Dear Reader,

I hope you enjoyed the second story of my Sisters Of The Heart series. In the first book of the series, *His Saving Grace,* Gracie finally woke up Jack, the man she'd loved for years, and, finally, he had enough sense to claim her as his own. At their wedding in the end of *Testing His Patience,* I introduced Connie, the third "sister of the heart." The final book will be her story. Look for *Loving Constance* in November 2004.

Gil and Patience carried a lot of "baggage." But the largest was a lack of forgiveness. It's hardest to forgive those who hurt us the most. However, we know we must forgive because Christ loved us first and forgave us. Forgiving isn't easy unless we remember that forgiving someone who has hurt us really frees us—once and for all—from the power of past pain. It brings hope and new life.

Forgiveness isn't saying wrong wasn't done; it's just letting go of our anger, cleaning it out of our lives and our souls. Let God take care of the reckoning, as in the Lord's Prayer—"Forgive us our trespasses as we forgive those who trespass against us." A tall order, but a necessary one.

Blessings,

Lyn Cote

ADAM'S PROMISE

BY

GAIL GAYMER MARTIN

Adam Montgomery was nurse Katherine Darling's worst nightmare—the arrogant surgeon in the Doctors Without Borders program had a good bedside manner with patients, not staff. But after several serious attempts on his life, Adam's gruffness softened under Kate's tender loving care. Would the transformed doctor be able to show Kate he needed her as a colleague...and a wife?

First book in the FAITH ON THE LINE series.

Don't miss

ADAM'S PROMISE

on sale July 2004

Available at your favorite retail outlet.